PUFF

Editor

MORE TELEVISION ADVENTURES OF WORZEL GUMMIDGE

Admirers of Worzel Gummidge, the irrepressible scarecrow of Scatterbrook Farm, will know by now that keeping the crows away from Ten-acre Field will never keep him out of trouble. In fact, there is no end to the predicaments he can get into, such as turning up at school in his Thinking Head and astonishing the staff with his great brain, or stowing away in a charabanc during the old people's outing, and being pursued by Saucy Nancy, who had spent most of her career as a ship's figurehead.

But the most important thing in Worzel's life is his devotion to that stiff-jointed little creature, Aunt Sally, however disdainfully she might treat him. And for her he even puts on his Gardening Head and tries to do an honest bit of work. Does he win her as his bride? Read through to the end of this new collection of hilarious stories and find out for yourself.

These new stories about Worzel have all appeared in the television series created by Keith Waterhouse and Willis Hall, who also wrote the first collection, *The Television Adventures of Worzel Gummidge*, and there are also three books about the original Worzel Gummidge by Barbara Euphan Todd, *Worzel Gummidge*, *Worzel Gummidge Again* and *Worzel Gummidge and Saucy Nancy*, which were written nearly forty years ago. You may be surprised to discover that in those days Aunt Sally was Worzel's aunt instead of his sweetheart, but then everything is always a bit unpredictable where Worzel is concerned . . .

KEITH WATERHOUSE
AND WILLIS HALL

More Television Adventures
of Worzel Gummidge

based on the characters created by

BARBARA EUPHAN TODD

PUFFIN BOOKS

Puffin Books, Penguin Books Ltd, Harmondsworth, Middlesex, England
Penguin Books, 625 Madison Avenue, New York, New York 10022, U.S.A.
Penguin Books Australia Ltd, Ringwood, Victoria, Australia
Penguin Books Canada Ltd, 2801 John Street, Markham, Ontario, Canada L3R 1B4
Penguin Books (N.Z.) Ltd, 182–190 Wairau Road, Auckland 10, New Zealand

—

Published in Puffin Books 1979

—

Copyright © Waterhall Worzel Ltd, 1979
All rights reserved

—

Made and printed in Great Britain
by Richard Clay (The Chaucer Press) Ltd,
Bungay, Suffolk
Set in Linotype Baskerville

Contents

CHAPTER I

The Saucy Nancy

ONE fine summer morning, when cherry blossom gusted like snow into the dense verges at the edge of the lane, and chattering flocks of goldfinches bounced on the heads of thistles, John and Sue Peters pouted irritably and argued with their father.

'*Why* can't we go, though, that's what I want to know?' asked John, petulantly.

'*Because* not,' his father answered irritatingly.

In the little lane outside Scatterbrook Farm Mr Peters was busy helping Mr Braithwaite, the farmer, and Dolly, his wife, load hampers of food and drink into a luggage hatch that ran along one side of a big blue coach. All the adults were dressed up; Mr Peters in his smartest check cap and a bright yellow waistcoat, the farmer in a tweed jacket and corduroy trousers and his jolly, beaming wife in a blue print frock covered with flowers, but while they looked happy and excited, the two children looked almost miserable.

'But children *always* go to the seaside,' Sue argued, scuffling her sandal in the dust.

Her father shook his head, 'Not this time. Just for once, the *grown-ups* go to the seaside and the *children* stay at home.'

'It's not fair,' Sue muttered, as Mrs Braithwaite

appeared at the gateway to the farmyard, adjusting her big floppy hat.

'Oh, give over grizzling, the pair of you!' she laughed. 'You wouldn't like it, even if you *did* come. Whoever heard of children on an old-age pensioners' outing!'

Mr Peters pushed the last of the picnic hampers deep into the recesses of the luggage compartment and straightened up with his hands on his back. 'I tell you what,' he offered magnanimously, 'I might bring you back a stick of rock!'

The children looked at one another sadly, then stared witheringly at their father. 'Big deal,' John muttered, turning away to toss a stone at a starling whistling at them from the top of one of the barns.

'What are *we* supposed to do all day long while you're off enjoying yourselves?' Sue demanded.

Mrs Braithwaite turned to reply as she clambered up the steps of the coach. 'There's a hundred and one things you can find to do on a farm!' she laughed. 'Go and look at that scarecrow.'

Mr Peters frowned as he slammed the doors of the luggage compartment. 'That'll take 'em all of two minutes!'

'Oh, they talk to that scarecrow for hours, Mr Peters,' the farmer's wife went on, as he climbed up into the driver's seat. 'Haven't you seen them? They make believe it's a friend of theirs.'

She leaned out of the window and called down to the children, 'Don't you, eh?'

John grinned, 'That's right –' he replied '– we call it Dad.'

'Cheeky monkey!' Mr Peters muttered as he started the engine.

A cloud of blue smoke poured out of the exhaust, the engine's roar startling the goldfinches into leaving their thistles and bouncing away over the hedge. The coach moved slowly forwards, leaving the children forlornly waving, 'Don't forget the rock,' called Sue.

As the roar of the engine died away, a robin peered down from the branch of a chestnut tree and sang cheerfully to the sad children.

John sighed. 'I think they're rotten.'

His sister studied a bright blue butterfly hovering over the grass verge. 'I suppose we *could* go and see Worzel,' she said unenthusiastically.

'If he's sulking again I'm not going to talk to him,' sniffed John as they set off down the lane.

'If he *is* sulking,' Sue pointed out, 'you wouldn't be able to!'

As they climbed the stile into Ten-acre Field a rabbit scuttled out of the hedge and dashed away in front of them. Sue balanced like a ballerina on top of the stile, watched it go, then turned to look for the scarecrow.

'I don't think he's there,' she said.

They climbed down and ran – not as fast as the rabbit – across the field to where the scarecrow pole stood. Sue was right: Worzel Gummidge wasn't there. 'Where do you think he's gone?' she wondered.

'How should I know?'

Sue bent down to pounce on something half-hidden in the long grass at the foot of the scarecrow pole.

'There!' she cried, triumphantly waving a bucket and spade. 'I'll give you three guesses where he's gone!'

By the time the two children had reached Ten-acre Field, the coach had reached the village and drawn up in the yard in front of the Crown Inn, where an eager crowd of old-age pensioners was pushing and jostling, anxious to be on board and away.

At the door of the coach Mr Peters, who had discovered a proper bus driver's peaked cap under the driving seat and put it on so that he looked the part, was taking tickets, while Mrs Braithwaite helped some of the older trippers to climb the steps. Mr Braithwaite did his best to form the noisy crowd into a queue, and he'd just about managed to get an orderly line organized when a turnippy face peered round the back of the coach.

'Oo-ah!' it breathed happily. A twiggy hand followed the face into view, then a broomhandle arm, a raggety old coat that might once have been black, and a pair of big black boots at the end of broomstick legs: Worzel Gummidge had come for the ride!

He waddled forward with his curious scarecrow walk, attached himself to the back of the queue, and suddenly slapped at his stomach. 'Dang Robin Redbreast!' he bellowed. 'Give over scritchin' an' scratchin'! Fair tickles me stomach, so 'e does, missus,' he said by way of explanation to an old lady who'd turned round and given him a nervous look. 'If you don't stop that flitterin' and flutterin',' he went on, as the old lady made her husband change places with her, 'you won't get to go on that see-saw!'

The old man in front of him gave him an odd look as they shuffled slowly forwards. 'See-saw? See-saw? You're a bit long in the tooth for riding on see-saws, aren't you?'

The scarecrow scowled at the old-age pensioner. 'What's wrong with you?' he snapped rudely. 'Silly ol' fool. We're *all* goin' on the see-saw, so we are! Oo-ah!'

The pensioner and his wife smiled at one another. 'All going on the see-saw?' the woman asked. 'What's he talking about? Does he mean the seaside?'

'He's a bit gaga,' her husband replied softly, turning to shout at Worzel Gummidge. 'We're going to the sea*side*!'

'No need to shout!' the scarecrow shouted back. 'I ain't deaf!'

'Well, then,' the woman chimed in, 'you know what the seaside is, don't you?'

'Course I do!' lied the scarecrow, who had very little idea what the seaside was! 'Been there 'undreds of times, so I 'ave. Every Christmas. Oo-ah! Allus 'ave my Christmas 'olidays on that there see-saw! Every year without fail.'

While they'd talked, the queue had shuffled forwards until all the other pensioners were on the coach. The couple in front of the scarecrow handed their tickets to Mr Peters, and Mrs Braithwaite helped them up the steps. Worzel Gummidge moved to follow them.

'Got your ticket?' asked Mr Peters breezily.

The scarecrow glared at him. 'What ticket?' he barked angrily. 'I don't need no ticket to go on the see-saw.'

Mrs Braithwaite shook her head, peering at Worzel Gummidge with a deep frown, trying to remember where she'd seen his face before. 'But you *do* need a ticket to get on the coach,' she said politely. 'Do you see? Didn't the Vicar give you one?'

On the coach, some of the pensioners were getting impatient, banging on the window with their walking sticks and gnashing their false teeth, eager to be off. Worzel Gummidge pulled an ugly face at them and answered Mrs Braithwaite. 'Vicar?' he said scornfully. 'Vicar wouldn't give me the time o' day, so 'e wouldn't.'

Mrs Braithwaite shook her head. 'Well, I'm sorry,' she said, 'but I'm afraid all the seats are booked.'

''Ow am I goin' to make a sand-pie, then?' demanded the scarecrow. 'Just answer me that. Can't make a sand-pie if I don't go on the see-saw. Stands to reason.'

'Sorry, grandpa,' said Mr Peters, moving down the steps to push him firmly but gently away. 'Better luck next time.'

For a moment there was a dangerous gleam in the scarecrow's eye, but Mr Peters stood his ground, and as a late-comer hobbled hurriedly towards the coach, brandishing his ticket, the scarecrow moved reluctantly aside to let him on.

'Fine parcel o' ol' crams this is, an' no mistake,' he

muttered angrily to himself. ''Ad my 'eart set on goin' on that there see-saw, so I did.'

He glanced back towards the coach door, where Mrs Braithwaite, bending with her back towards him, was giving the late-comer a heave up the steps. The gleam flashed back into the scarecrow's eye and he raised a boot ready to give her a hearty kick up the backside.

'Oi!' called Mr Peters, who'd decided it would be a good idea to keep an eye on him. 'That'll do, grandpa. Off you go now.'

Worzel Gummidge snarled angrily at him, but in the moment while Mr Peters had distracted his attention Mrs Braithwaite had straightened up and climbed aboard.

'Bloomin' pesky ol' bus,' he muttered grumpily as he wandered round the back of the coach. ''Oo wants to go on your bloomin' pesky ol' bus anyway?'

To make up for not having been able to kick Mrs Braithwaite's bottom he kicked the back tyre of the coach instead, and wandered on to kick the other one. 'Good mind to let all their tyres down, so I 'ave,' he told himself. 'Serve 'em all right, so it would, the whole pack an' parcel of 'em.'

He gave the other back tyre a hearty boot and found himself on the far side of the coach, where Mr Braithwaite was loading crates of ale from the pub into the gaping luggage compartment. The scarecrow's eyes lit up, and he watched quietly as the farmer finished his task and strolled round the front of the coach to talk to Mr Peters.

'Oo-ah,' he murmured with delight as he stared into

the darkness where the hampers and crates of ale were stored. 'All them seats is booked, is they? Need a ticket, do I? Well, stands to reason I don't need no ticket to get in this 'ere 'ole, 'cos there ain't no seats in 'ere, so there ain't,' he argued, climbing awkwardly in to hide himself carefully behind the hampers, just a moment before Mr Braithwaite returned to slam the door shut.

There was a muffled, distant cheer, then a roaring noise as Mr Peters started the engine, and a bounce that set the robin fluttering in his stomach: they were on their way!

Under the bright sunshine of a beautiful summer day the coach crawled slowly along the narrow, winding lanes that led out of the village, then gradually began to gather speed as it turned into a better road.

In the driving seat, under his peaked cap, Mr Peters was enjoying himself hugely, and behind him, in the coach, Mrs Braithwaite busied herself making sure all the pensioners were comfortable, tucking rugs around their legs and handing round boiled sweets, while her husband told jokes to keep everyone amused and pointed out famous landmarks as they sped past.

Everyone was happy; the trip to the seaside had begun perfectly, but if any of them had realized what was happening beneath their feet there would have been an uproar!

For below, in the darkness of the luggage compartment, Worzel Gummidge had started to investigate the contents of the picnic hamper.

'Oo-ah!' he growled, delighted with what he found.

'Chicken legs. An' san'wiches. An' a nice bit o' 'am. An' some biled eggs. Oo-ah! I likes a biled egg, so I do! This is goin' to be a rare ol' feast for a scarecrow, an' no mistake!'

There was a jolt as the coach stopped. The scarecrow pushed open the door of the luggage compartment and peered out.

In front of the coach there was a closed level crossing gate where a sleepy little train was puffing lazily past, as if it wasn't really too sure where it was supposed to be going or too bothered about when it got there, and beside the coach, only a yard away from Worzel Gummidge's hiding place, a farm labourer leaned on a bicycle, waiting patiently for the gate to open.

'Oi! Is this 'ere the see-saw?' croaked the scarecrow.

The labourer jumped, turned in surprise, and caught sight of Worzel Gummidge.

'Eh? This is Little Smattering Halt, this is,' he replied.

'Ar. Well. In that case, is it dinner time yet?'

'It's only 'alf past nine!'

The scarecrow nodded contentedly. 'Near enough. Oo-ah!'

As the train disappeared and the gate opened the scarecrow slammed the luggage compartment door shut again, leaving the farm labourer standing open-mouthed, scratching his head and staring at the back of the coach as it pulled away down the road.

For an hour the coach rolled through beautiful

countryside, past green fields and over rivers, through thick woods and sleepy villages full of thatched cottages. And all through the beautiful countryside, the coach left behind it a trail of crisp packets, chicken legs, orange peel, egg shells, sandwich crusts, cheese wrappers, ginger beer bottles, apple cores and fizzy drink cans, for in the luggage compartment Worzel Gummidge was feasting on the contents of the picnic hampers, tossing out what he didn't want or couldn't eat onto the road from time to time.

His meal left him sleepy, and for the last part of the journey he dozed off, only to awaken with a start to find the coach coming to a standstill and a familiar harsh sound penetrating his scarecrow dreams.

'What? What?' he barked, throwing open the door of the luggage compartment and staring angrily up at the sky. 'Tarnation rooks, wakin' a body up! I'll give 'ee what for, with your cawin' an' croakin'!' He caught sight of the noisy bird wheeling above the coach and frowned. 'Oo-ah, 'tain't a rook at all, so it ain't. Not unless 'e's fallen in a sack of flour. 'Tis one 'o them there dangnation gulls, what drops fishbones down scarecrowses necks when they ain't lookin'. Oo-ah! That's a gull right enough. So this must be the seesaw. Stands to reason!'

He stretched elaborately, filled his pockets with the few odd scraps of food that he hadn't yet eaten, climbed out of the luggage compartment and gazed about him. The coach was parked right on the harbour's edge, near a tiny pier which housed a little amusement arcade. There was a tang of salt sea on the air, and the hiss of surf on the shingle.

The scarecrow wandered round the back of the coach and sat on the bollard by the pier, listening with interest as Mrs Braithwaite spoke to the pensioners straggling slowly off the bus.

'Could I have your attention, everybody?' she called. 'As it's getting on for twelve o'clock, we thought we'd go straight down to the beach and have our picnic. Could I have volunteers to carry the hampers?'

A couple of the more agile pensioners scuttled round the coach, calling over their shoulders as they went. 'Leave it to us, Mrs Braithwaite. Long as we get extra rations!' cried one.

'I'll carry the beer crates!' said the other.

Mr Peters nudged the farmer's wife. 'Mention about the baccy, Mrs Braithwaite.'

She snapped her fingers as she remembered. 'I nearly forgot. There's half an ounce of tobacco for everyone who smokes. And boiled sweets and fruit for those who don't.'

'Come on now,' called Mr Peters. 'Down to the beach. See if we can't find a nice sheltered spot out of the wind.'

As the pensioners picked their way down the damp concrete steps onto the beach, Mr Peters caught sight of Worzel Gummidge, squatting on his bollard and eating a banana. He nudged Mrs Braithwaite. 'Hey! Isn't that the chap who tried to cadge a ride with us this morning?'

She shook her head. 'It can't be. Not unless he's flown here.'

As they talked, the two men who had gone to collect the picnics heaved their hampers and looked puzzled.

'This one's not very heavy, Colin. What's in it? A batch of fairy cakes?'

'It's not *my* missus's baking, that's for sure,' Colin replied.

The scarecrow watched with amusement as they put down the hampers and lifted the lids. 'Hey! Look at this!' Colin shouted, fishing out an apple core and the remains of a well-chewed chicken leg. The other pensioner stared aghast at a half-eaten pork pie and an empty crisp packet. They began frantically hauling the other hampers out of the luggage compartment, opening each one as it tumbled to the ground.

'It's gone!' they gasped in astonishment. 'All of it! The whole blessed picnic!' and they stared around them to see the scarecrow ambling along the sea front with a half-eaten apple in one hand and in the other an iced bun with a large bite taken out of it.

'Seagulls!' called Worzel Gummidge knowledge-ably to the two old men.

They looked at one another in bewilderment. 'Sea-gulls?' they echoed.

The scarecrow nodded solemnly. 'Oo-ah! Thievin' varmints, so they are. You take a tip from me. Watch out for a seagull with cake-crumbs on its beak,' and tossing his apple core with a plop into the sea he wandered happily on his way.

Behind him the two pensioners looked at one another, then hurried away to break the awful news to Mr Peters and Mrs Braithwaite.

Worzel Gummidge decided he liked the seaside.

There were no rooks to be seen, so he had no work to do, and he rather enjoyed the fresh smell of salt and seaweed that rose from the beach as he strolled along by the harbour wall. There were cheerful noises of people enjoying themselves coming from the little amusement arcade on the pier, and a handful of fishing boats bobbed on the water, half a mile out to sea.

As he took in the sights and sounds of the seaside, his eye fell on an ancient fishing vessel moored a few yards away, and he strolled closer to make out its name – *The Saucy Nancy* – painted in bright red in curling script on the bow. There was a carved wooden figure-head on the ship, a big buxom lady in flowing diaphanous robes the colour of damp seaweed, her brawny arms folded across her chest, and on the harbour wall, beside a notice that read TOUR OF HISTORIC WHALER 10p sat an old salt with a black eye patch, a wooden leg and a gaily-coloured parrot on his shoulder.

'Who'll come aboard *The Saucy Nancy*?' he called, rather forlornly, for no one was listening to him. 'Ten Pence. See round the 'istoric whaler. 'Ere you are, matey,' he brightened, catching sight of Worzel Gummidge, ''Ave your photo took with *The Saucy Nancy*. Ten Pence only.'

'Is this 'ere a ship?' demanded the scarecrow.

'What's it look like? A bloomin' telephone kiosk?' replied the old salt rather sharply. 'Ten Pence!' he insisted as the scarecrow tried to peer in through a porthole.

Worzel Gummidge considered the offer. 'Ten Pence, eh? Where's it goin'?'

'*She* ain't goin' nowhere,' frowned the old salt.

The scarecrow sniffed. 'Just as well, 'cos I ain't got ten pence.'

'Then push off,' growled the old salt, but Worzel Gummidge was in no hurry.

He stared down at the man. 'That's a fine wooden leg you got there, mister sailorman,' he commented. 'You ain't been a scarecrow in your time, by any happy chance?'

The old salt looked annoyed. 'I'm warning you – push off!'

' 'Cos if you does chance to be a scarecrow, you ain't much good at scarin' seagulls, is you?' he went on, pointing at the brightly-coloured parrot on the sailor's shoulder.

The parrot screeched with laughter, making the sailor jump. 'What're you laughing at?' he demanded.

'He's laughin' at you, you silly old lummock,' the scarecrow answered. 'Call yourself a scarecrow? There's that red an' blue seagull just sittin' there laughin' 'is 'ead off!'

The old salt's face went as red as the parrot's. 'If you don't push off you'll feel the toe of my boot!' he barked.

The scarecrow stood his ground. 'That's as may be,' he replied evenly. 'Anyone kicks Worzel, 'e gets kicked right back again! Oo-ah! You see if 'e don't!'

The parrot gave another screeching laugh and the old salt shouted at it angrily. 'One more squawk out of you and I'll put a bag over your head!'

Bored with the conversation, Worzel Gummidge

strolled off along the quay while the old salt glowered at his back. In a moment, as the scarecrow neared a fisherman, the old salt took a crafty look round and, when he was sure no one was watching, whipped off his eye-patch and his fake wooden leg, stretched out his real leg and sauntered casually off to the pub for lunch.

'Mornin',' said the scarecrow to the fisherman. 'Why for you 'oldin' that there pole out?'

The fisherman shifted on his little folding stool and slowly turned his head to look up at the scarecrow with an expression of contempt. 'I'm trying to signal a taxi, aren't I?' he sighed.

Worzel Gummidge shook his head. Little dollops of mud that had dried out in the warm luggage compartment fell to the ground. 'Funny lot, you see-saw folk. You're all half barmy if you axe me.'

The fisherman sniffed and turned back to watch his float. 'You're bothering me,' he called over his shoulder. 'Clear off!'

The float bobbed suddenly in the blue water. The fisherman jumped up and eagerly began to wind in his reel, leaning forward over the harbour wall as he did so. The scarecrow eyed the tempting target of the fisherman's broad backside, licked his lips, stepped back a pace, lined himself up and swung back his boot.

'Waaaaak! 'Oo's a pretty boy then? 'Oo's a pretty boy then?' screamed the parrot from his perch on the bollard by *The Saucy Nancy*. The startled fisherman swung round.

'What are you up to?' he demanded, eyeing the scarecrow's uplifted leg.

Worzel Gummidge examined his boot with interest, as if it were the first time he'd set eyes on it. 'Nothing, mister,' he lied. 'Ain't doing nothing,' and he strolled casually away to glower at the parrot. He looked cross and spiteful as he bent down to berate the bird. 'If it 'adn't been for you I could've kicked 'im into the water. Oo-ah! 'Ad 'im lined up, so I did. Bang in front o' the toe o' me boot.'

'Ahoy there!' called a fruity voice.

The scarecrow scowled at the parrot. ''Oy yourself, you bloomin' rainbow-coloured seagull!' He stretched out his broomhandle arms and adopted his official crowscaring position. 'Go on! Shoo! Get off out of it!'

'Ahoy there!' came the fruity voice again.

'I'll not tell 'ee aga –'

The scarecrow broke off and bent forward, frowning, to look closely at the parrot. 'Now that's funny,' he muttered, puzzled. ''Ow come you can talk without your beak movin'? Come to think on it, 'ow come you can talk at all, you just bein' a stewpid ol' bird?' He straightened up and scratched his head.

'It's not him, you turnip-headed landlubber!' roared the fruity voice. 'It's me! Behind you!' and a horny hand tapped him on the shoulder. The scarecrow jumped a foot in the air and turned to find behind him the figurehead of *The Saucy Nancy*, her muscular arms folded across her deep chest and a broad smile on her weather-beaten mahogany face.

'Well, I'll go to market in a basket o' duck eggs!' exclaimed Worzel Gummidge, flabbergasted.

Saucy Nancy looked him up and down. 'Before you does, 'ave you got any tobaccy?' she asked.

The scarecrow nodded, 'As a matter o' fact I 'ave. Found it tucked away in a picnic basket, so I did. It don't taste very nice, though,' he added, handing over one of the store of half-ounces Mr Braithwaite had hidden away for the pensioners. Saucy Nancy's eyes lit up, and her huge smile spread even wider as she delved deeply into the folds of her robe and dragged out a battered old corn-cob pipe.

'Tastes nice enough if you chews it proper,' she growled, taking the packet from Worzel Gummidge and sniffing deeply at it. She rolled the tobacco between her palms and began to stuff her pipe carefully, making sure it was neither too tight nor too loose. 'But I don't chew it,' she went on, 'I smokes it.' She deftly struck a match against her wooden hip and lit the pipe, puffing out great clouds of smoke into the alarmed scarecrow's face.

'You don't want to be doin' that, missus,' said Worzel Gummidge nervously, stepping back a pace. 'Set yourself afire so you will! Oo-ah!' A thought struck him, and he frowned. ''Ere, 'Ow come you can talk yakkity like what yewmans do?'

Saucy Nancy puffed her pipe contentedly and gave a slow smile. 'The Crowman learned me, o' course,' she said in a soft, deep murmur.

The scarecrow removed his hat reverently and bowed his head for a moment at the mention of the

Crowman's name. 'Oo-ah! I didn't know as you'd
'ad the privilege an' the pleasure o' meetin' 'is 'igh an'
mightiness. But why for the Crowman made you talk,
eh? You ain't no scarecrow!'

Saucy Nancy pulled a long face and examined the
bowl of her pipe thoughtfully. 'I was going to be,' she
said sadly. 'After our last voyage. They was going to
put me on the allotments, for to keep the gulls off of
the radishes.' Her eyes lit up as she remembered. 'Then
the captin says, no, he says, blow me down, he says, I'll
keep her here, he says! And here I am!' She sucked
contentedly on her yellow corn-cob pipe and nodded
happily. 'Shiver me timbers, but this is good baccy!
Got any more?' she asked hopefully.

The scarecrow narrowed his eyes. 'I might have. I
might not. Depends on what *you* got.'

Saucy Nancy thought for a moment, then dug deep
into the folds of her costume and hauled out a
crumpled paper bag. ''Umbugs?' she offered.

Worzel Gummidge smacked his lips. ''Umbugs!
Oo-ah! Now I likes 'umbugs, so I do!'

He crammed a handful of humbugs into his mouth
and munched contentedly as Saucy Nancy drew long
pulls on her pipe. At their back the sea sighed on the
shingle and strands of seaweed the same wet, dark
green as Saucy Nancy's skirt swam slowly to and fro.

'Well now,' said the figurehead suddenly after a
long silence. 'With my 'umbugs and your baccy we
makes a fine pair. 'Ow about you an' me gettin' married?'

'Married?' The scarecrow had a sudden coughing

fit as a humbug went down the wrong way. 'Gettin' married?' he spluttered agitatedly. 'I can't marry you, missus! I'm spoken for!'

Saucy Nancy let out a long, screeching laugh, rather like the parrot. '*Spoken* for?' she bellowed, 'Who'd have you? 'Cept me, that is!'

Worzel Gummidge recovered his breath and his composure. 'Aunt Sally,' he said proudly. 'That's 'oo'd 'ave me. If I knowed where she's got to. I think she went to Runamia. Else Egypt.'

Saucy Nancy shook her head. 'No, she ain't there, dearie, 'cos I been there and I'd've seen her. Been all over, I have. Iceland ... Denmark ... Portsmouth. And I 'aven't seen her nowhere. She's probably drownded. So you might as well marry your Saucy Nancy.'

The scarecrow's desperation showed in his quavering voice as he tried to think of ways out of his problem. 'You don't want to marry me, missus! I'm too stewpid. In fact, I'll tell you 'ow stewpid ol' Worzel Gummidge is. When I first 'eard you talk I thought it was that there coloured seagull! That's 'ow stewpid I am! Thinkin' seagulls can talk!' and he reached out an arm to point to the parrot.

'Pretty Polly!' cried the bird, running up the scarecrow's arm to perch on his shoulder. 'Pretty Polly! Who's a pretty boy then?'

Defeated, the scarecrow glared at the happy bird. 'Who axed *you* to chime in?' he demanded glumly.

While Worzel Gummidge was being argued into marriage by Saucy Nancy, a crocodile of gloomy pensioners was trailing after Mr and Mrs Braithwaite and Mr Peters, grumbling about their lost lunch and looking thoroughly miserable as they made their way along the little pier to the amusement arcade.

'I'm starving, Mr Peters,' muttered the farmer angrily as they passed the rifle range. 'If I get my hands on the scallywag who stole our lunches I'll throttle him!'

Mr Peters looked up to where a young man was putting the last touches to the painted sign over the coconut shy. 'No use crying over spilt milk, Mr Braithwaite,' he replied with forced cheerfulness, 'We'll just have to find somewhere that serves food.'

'What, a café, you mean?' joined in Mrs Braithwaite, who was as hungry as her husband.

Mr Peters looked back along the pier to where an inn sign dangled invitingly from a pub on the sea front. 'Well,' he said, 'not necessarily a café. Shall I explore?' and he would have been off up the pier in a trice if Mrs Braithwaite hadn't tugged at his sleeve.

'Look!' she whispered urgently, 'Do you see what I see?'

Frowning, Mr Peters followed her pointing finger and stared at the coconut-shy. It was the very start of the seaside season, and the shy was still only half-painted, with dirty brown streaks of years-old paint alongside bright new panels of red and blue and green. On a ladder, the young man with the paint brush was now slapping great wild daubs of green across the fascia.

'I can't see anything. What am I supposed to be

looking at, anyway?' said Mr Peters, anxious to get away and examine the pub.

She took his hand and led him closer.

The proprietor of the shy, busy unpacking wooden balls from a tea-chest, saw them coming and at once switched on his professional smile.

'Roll up there!' he cried. 'Five balls five pence. One penny per ball is all you pay to win any prize.' He looked up at the lad with the paint brush and frowned. 'Hurry up with that ladder, Percy! You're in this gentleman's way.'

'Oh, it's all right,' said Mr Peters quickly, 'We're just looking.'

Suddenly losing interest in them, the proprietor moved away and wandered to the back of the coconut-shy. Mr Peters stared. A line of smart new Aunt Sallies stared blankly back at him.

'There!' said Mrs Braithwaite, 'Can't you see? That Aunt Sally in the middle – is it or isn't it the Aunt Sally that Mr Shepherd used to own?'

Mr Peters cocked his head on one side and pursed his lips as he examined the single, bedraggled, dirty old figure with the peeling paint that stood in the middle of the row. 'Could be,' he admitted. 'He might have sold it.'

'He didn't *sell* it, Mr Peters,' scolded Mrs Braithwaite, 'it was stolen. He had it in a trunk in his attic – and one day he went up there and it had walked!'

Mr Peters caught sight of the young lad, who had come down from his ladder and was standing nearby, listening and scowling. He flapped a warning finger at

Mrs Braithwaite. 'I wouldn't make any accusations, Mrs Braithwaite,' he whispered nervously. 'They can turn very nasty, these fairground people. Come on, let's explore the food situation.'

The young man watched them walk away and called to his boss. 'All done, guv.'

'Very nice, Percy,' agreed the proprietor as he strolled out to inspect the young man's handiwork. 'Just like new.'

'Shall I tell you what lets it down, guv?' the young man went on, 'That old Aunt Sally. The one in the middle. She looks a right mess.'

'So would you if you'd been fished out of the sea! She just needs a lick of paint, that's all.'

The young man waved his pot of green paint eagerly. 'No problem, guv,' he cried, heading for the back of the stall.

'Not *you*, Percy! It's a craftsman's job,' explained the proprietor of the shy. 'That chap who paints the Carousel, he'll do it. Dump her in that tea-chest and I'll take her round tonight.'

Resignedly, the young man put down his pot of paint, slung Aunt Sally over his shoulder and carted her off round the back of the stall.

On the quayside, Worzel Gummidge and Saucy Nancy were strolling along arm-in-arm. The figure-head was still puffing contentedly on her corn-cob pipe, but the scarecrow was looking positively irritable.

'I say, missus,' he began.

'Yes, dearie?'

'Why for is you hangin' hold o' my arm? You ain't goin' to fall down, is you?'

Saucy Nancy smiled a slow smile, took her pipe out of her mouth and answered him mysteriously in a deep, mellow voice. 'Ah! That's as may be! I ain't got no legs, see!'

The scarecrow snorted. 'Course you got legs, missus! Everybody's got legs. 'Ceptin' worms, an' they don't need 'em.'

'Neither does figureheads,' replied Saucy Nancy reasonably. 'Lash you to the prow of a schooner in a North Sea gale and *you* wouldn't need no legs neither. 'Ceptin' sea-legs, that is!' She gave a screeching force ten laugh at her own joke, and Worzel Gummidge winced.

He looked at her sharply. ''Ow does you get about then, if you ain't got legs?'

The figurehead dropped her eyes modestly, and it seemed as though the hint of a blush spread over her already deep mahogany face. 'Well,' she whispered, 'I shouldn't really show you till we're married, but when I comes ashore I 'as these, see?' and she shyly hitched up her skirt to reveal that she was mounted on a set of old pram wheels.

The scarecrow's mouth gaped open in astonishment. 'Well!' he gasped. 'I'll go lie down in a trough o' sheep dip!'

Saucy Nancy dropped her damp, seaweed-green skirt again and lowered her eyes with a bashful little giggle. 'You'll *have* to marry me now,' she simpered.

'You're half-barmy, missus,' snorted the scarecrow,

'that's what you are. I keeps tellin' you – I's goin' to marry Aunt Sally!'

'And I keeps telling *you* that you can't, 'cos she's drownded. So give me one good reason why you shouldn't marry your Saucy Nancy,' she scolded.

Worzel Gummidge considered the problem. 'You're ugly,' he decided.

'Do you think so?' she said brightly. 'Thank you! So are you.'

'An' you smells of fish,' he went on.

'Course I smells o' fish! You'd smell o' fish if you'd served all your life afore the mast! Anyway,' she said stubbornly, 'what's wrong with a bit o' fish?' Her voice dropped still lower and became seductive. 'I expect you wouldn't say no to a few whelks and a pint o' winkles, eh?'

The scarecrow's eyes widened. 'That I wouldn't, missus,' he agreed.

'Well, then. *I* knows where there's a whelk stall.'

Arm-in-arm they lurched off, the scarecrow with his strange staggering gait and Saucy Nancy rattling bumpily along beside him on her pram wheels. Along the quayside they went, round the curve of harbour where the fishing boats swung lazily on long ropes, and lines of gulls sat silent in the sun, to the end of the stubby little pier with its tired old amusements.

Saucy Nancy led the scarecrow past the roundabout, past the rifle range, almost to the end of the pier, where the sea grumbled and heaved beneath their feet, until they rounded a corner and came on the tantalizing smell of cockles and winkles, mussels and shrimps and prawns. The owner of the stall spotted them coming and made a grab for the plate of whelks as Worzel Gummidge dived in.

'Not so fast!' he barked at the scarecrow. 'Money first!'

'Money. Ar. See, the thing is, mister, they won't give me no wages –'

'I've got money, cap'n,' Saucy Nancy chipped in, delving deep into the recesses of her flowing robes and slapping a strange-looking foreign coin on the counter. 'An' keep the change,' she added generously.

The whelk stall owner examined it suspiciously, sniffed at it, held it up to the light, bit it. 'What's this?'

'A Spanish doubloon, cap'n! Found it in a treasure chest, fifteen fathoms down ...'

The whelk stall owner tossed it back at her. 'I don't take foreign coins,' he informed her dourly. 'Go on, sling your hooks! Oi, you!' he bellowed as Worzel Gummidge grabbed a handful of whelks and crammed them into his mouth. 'Get your thievin' hands off!'

The scarecrow put his shoulder to the figurehead and wheeled her quickly away round the side of the stall as the angry stall-holder set off after them. They doubled back, twice round the roundabout and all along the pier, and were just about to escape round the back of the coconut-shy when the scarecrow stopped dead in his tracks, gaping in surprise at a pair of legs sticking up into the air from a tea-chest.

'Why're we hove to, shipmate?' asked Saucy Nancy.

''Alf a tick, missus,' replied Worzel Gummidge, 'I'd recognize them ankles anywhere.'

Saucy Nancy shook her head. 'You don't need ankles at a time like this, me hearty! What you need is a good pair of wheels!'

'Don't argufy, missus,' said Worzel Gummidge, grabbing hold of one of the protruding legs. 'Get 'old an' 'eave!'

She did as she was told, and with a great tug they yanked Aunt Sally out of the tea-chest and stood her on her feet. She didn't look at all grateful.

'This is *too* much!' she exclaimed. 'That common old Scarecrow again! Let me go at once or I'll pull your stupid head off!'

'Time for fun an' games later, Aunt Sally,' said the scarecrow seriously. 'We've gotta run for it,' and taking one elbow each, he and Saucy Nancy propelled Aunt Sally away down the pier just as the whelk stall owner appeared, with the proprietor of the coconut-shy at his side.

'There they are!' yelled the angry whelk stall man.

'What are you doing with my Aunt Sally! Come here, you!' shouted the other as they galloped away down the pier in hot pursuit.

With all his usual cunning, the scarecrow steered his two companions down alleyways and through arches until they were deep into the little fishing village and well away from the quay, their pursuers far behind and quite lost. Saucy Nancy produced a beautiful little folding brass telescope from her billowing gown and peered back along the way they'd come.

'We shook 'em off, shipmates,' she announced happily. 'They're heading nor-nor-west.'

Aunt Sally glared at Worzel Gummidge. 'I suppose you expect me to be grateful?'

'Course I expects 'ee to be grateful, Aunt Sally. We got 'ee out o' that there coakienut-shy, didn't we?'

'Yes, and look at me,' she snapped. 'My beautiful face all chipped. If it hadn't been for your interference, I'll have you know, I was about to be repainted by the man who paints the carousel! You've spoiled everything, as per usual!'

Saucy Nancy looked with amusement at the angry Aunt Sally. 'You could do with your barnacles scraping, dearie,' she smiled. 'What you been doin' in the briny?'

Aunt Sally cut her dead with a look and turned to speak to the scarecrow. 'I don't know who this person is,' she said as snootily as ever Mrs Bloomsbury-Barton could, 'but if it's any of her business, it just so happens that I was floating to Egypt. To marry an Egyptian prince, you know. Only some interferin' busybody came along an' fished me out with an 'ook! Next thing I knew, they was throwin' wooden balls at my 'ead,' she finished, her snooty accent slipping as she recalled her fate.

'Never mind, Aunt Sally,' said the scarecrow comfortingly, 'you's safe again, now.'

The scarecrow spoke too soon. As they wandered through the back streets of the little fishing village their route brought them out into the street where the pensioners' outing had found a café for lunch, and at the very moment that Worzel Gummidge was reassuring Aunt Sally, Mrs Braithwaite was frowning and nudging Mr Peters.

'Hey, isn't that him?'

Mr Peters squinted across the street. 'Are you sure? He didn't have those two funny-looking women with him.'

But the pensioners were sure!

'It *is* him, Mister Peters!' one of them shouted. 'Come on lads! That's the thieving vagabond who pinched our picnics!'

'Oo-ah!' murmured Worzel Gummidge apprehensively as the crowd of angry pensioners levered themselves stiffly out of their seats and began to hobble across the road, waving their walking sticks threateningly.

'Daisies an' buttercups! They runs around like mad bullocks!' he gasped, and once again grabbing the reluctant Aunt Sally by the elbows, they began to bolt for it.

The little fishing village was a maze of winding streets and twisting alleyways, and the trio had to weave around like Mad March Hares to escape. Once, just as they thought they'd escaped from the pensioners, they turned a corner to find themselves face to face with the angry whelk stall owner and the man who ran the coconut-shy, and had to double back and run even faster.

At last, they emerged into a quiet square where a few of the villagers were sunning themselves at tables outside a tiny pub. Worzel Gummidge breathed a sigh of relief and Saucy Nancy took out her pipe again, glancing longingly across at the pub.

'Well, shipmates,' she suggested, 'what about a tot o' rum?'

There wasn't even time for Aunty Sally to give her a withering reply before a shout came from the pub as a sailor glanced across the square and spotted them.

'Captain!' he shouted. 'That there's your figurehead off of *The Saucy Nancy*, ain't it?'

The old salt's eyes popped, and he spilled his beer as he jumped to his feet. 'It bloomin' is!' he muttered, setting off across the square with a couple of his mates at his heels.

The fugitive trio looked at one another with alarm and began to gallop away, cutting up a narrow little path between two rows of tall houses just as Mr Peters and Mrs Braithwaite led the pensioners into the square from one end, and the whelk stall owner and the coconut-shy man raced in from the other. In a minute the quiet little square was a madhouse, with pensioners and fishermen and fairgroundmen hopelessly entangled, pushing and shoving one another in their frantic attempts to find out which way their quarry had gone.

By the time they'd sorted themselves out, Worzel Gummidge, Saucy Nancy and Aunt Sally were well away and had made it to the safety of a tiny park on top of a hill overlooking the little fishing village.

'Funny 'ow these yewman beings carry on, ain't it shipmates?' mused Saucy Nancy speculatively, as she lit her pipe once more.

Aunt Sally sniffed snootily. 'They're not well-bred, that's their trouble.'

'It's this 'ere see-saw they lives in,' said the scarecrow. 'They're all barmy.'

Saucy Nancy looked around at the park. 'Well, me hearties, what shall we do now?'

'We?' said Aunt Sally, affronted, '*We? Aye* don't see any *we. Aye* only see my beautiful self and a dirty old scarecrow.'

'She's just 'avin' 'er little joke,' explained the scarecrow. 'She sees you all right. She might'a lost 'er paint but she ain't gone cross-eyed.'

'*You* don't seem to understand the rules of polite society,' insisted Aunt Sally. 'If you'd been brought up proper, you'd know that this person does not ... *H*exist until she 'as been ... *H*introduced. So go on, you stupid hank of straw. Hintroduce us!'

The scarecrow took off his hat and did the job properly. 'Aunt Sally. This 'ere's Saucy Nancy. Saucy Nancy, this 'ere's Aunt Sally.'

'Pleased to meet you, I'm sure.'

'Likewise, dearie,' replied the figurehead.

Aunt Sally gave her a condescending smile. 'And who were your family, may I ask? Did you fall out of a basket of clothes pegs when you were little, or was you made by a humble woodcarver what was learning his trade?'

'*My* family, dearie,' said Saucy Nancy firmly, 'goes back to the Vikings. See this face o' mine? It's been handed on down through the ages.'

Aunt Sally sneered. 'Yes, it looks it.'

'Well, at least it *is* a face, dearie,' said Saucy Nancy, getting her own back. 'It's never been mistaken for the back of a puddin' spoon, unlike *some* faces not a 'undred nautical miles from here.'

Aunt Sally stamped her foot. 'Worzel!' she demanded, 'I refuse to stand here and be insulted by this ... by this piece of *driftwood*! Take me home at once!'

'Home, Aunt Sally? 'Oo's 'ome?'

She looked at him witheringly. 'You stupid, ignorant scarecrow! Your home, of course! You don't think I want to go back to that common fairground, do you? New coat of paint or *no* new coat of paint!'

The scarecrow's face was wreathed in a rapturous smile. 'Back to my 'ome!' he breathed. 'If you knew 'ow I've longed to 'ear them words from your lips, Aunt Sally! I *will* take you back to my 'ome, 'umble though it is. An' you shall 'ave the best chair. An' the best sack o' potaties to sleep on. An' tomorrow mornin' I shall axe the Crowman to marry us, an' then we'll be Mister an' Missus Worzel Gummidge!'

'Yes, well, we'll talk about that later,' said Aunt Sally dismissively. 'Come along.'

She took the scarecrow's arm, and was about to move away with him when Saucy Nancy suddenly wheeled herself in front of them. 'Hold hard, me hearties!' she growled, folding her knotty arms. 'Where do you think you're going?'

Worzel Gummidge shuffled nervously from foot to foot. 'Back to Scatterbrook, for to get married,' he explained. 'It was very nice meetin' you, Saucy Nancy. My pleasure.'

'I see. So now you want to cast me away like a broken lobster pot. Is that it?'

Aunt Sally sneered. 'There *is* a resemblance, now that you mention it.'

Saucy Nancy stood her ground and puffed smoke into Aunt Sally's face. 'I wasn't talking to you, you fossilized door-knocker. But now that I *am* talking to you, I'll have you know that this 'ere scarecrow ... *H*appens to be my ... *H*intended!'

Aunt Sally stuck her painted nose in the air. 'Don't be ridiculous.'

'That's right, what Aunt Sally says,' said Worzel quickly, 'it's ridickerluss. I telled 'ee all along – I'm spoken for.'

Saucy Nancy snorted derisively. 'Spoken for, is you? You wasn't spoken for when you et all my humbugs, was you?'

The scarecrow patted his stomach. 'You can 'ave your 'umbugs back, Saucy Nancy. They're all 'ere in my stummick.'

'How disgusting!' said Aunt Sally.

Saucy Nancy prodded Aunt Sally with the stem of her corn-cob pipe. 'If my intended wants to be disgusting he'll *be* disgusting. So keep your long flaking nose out of it.'

'At least I haven't got death-watch beetle in my nose, like some I could mention. Come on Worzel, we're going home.'

'That we are, Aunt Sally,' he agreed fervently. 'Good arternoon, missus.'

'Oh no you ain't!' insisted Saucy Nancy firmly. 'I'm telling you for the last time. He's *mine!*'

She grabbed the scarecrow's free arm and began to heave on it as if she were pulling up an anchor chain.

'Let go of him!' yelled Aunt Sally, pulling him back by the other arm, 'He's mine!'

'Mine!' they yelled, 'Mine!' heaving and hauling the worried scarecrow this way and that, backwards and forwards between them so violently that tufts of straw began to come loose.

''Ere! Mind my straw!' he cried nervously. 'You'll pull me to pieces, so you will! Let go me arms! I'm coming to bits! Look,' he offered in despair, 'let me go an' I'll marry both of 'ee! Now you've done it!' he cried as the two females fell back clutching handfuls of straw.

'Heeeeeelp!' he croaked, making off down the hill as fast as his legs would carry him.

'Wait for me, shipmate!' cried the figurehead.

There was a nasty gleam in Aunt Sally's eye. 'Oh, you want to go after him, do you? Then so you shall!' and she gave Saucy Nancy a heave that sent her rolling after the scarecrow, her wheels spinning.

In the fishing village, the pensioners and the sailors, the whelk stall owner and the coconut-shy man, Mr Peters and Mrs Braithwaite had all untangled themselves and made their way together to the little inn overlooking the harbour, and were stretched out on benches and in chairs, drinking in the peaceful scene. A line of gulls watched from the harbour wall, waiting for the pickings from pork pies and sandwiches.

Above them, a bright sun beamed cheerfully down, and the rich warm smell of damp seaweed drifted across to them from the highwater mark. At the pub door, with several sticks of rock under his arm, Mr Peters stood up and turned to Mrs Braithwaite.

'Time we were moving, I think,' he began, then broke off in amazement. He stared along the quay to the little street at the end where Saucy Nancy was careering into view at a terrible pace.

'Look out, everybody!' he bellowed, and dived for cover as the figurehead, its pram wheels protesting squeakily, rattled along the quayside, over the cobbles, and straight in through the front door of the pub, where it came to a stop against the bar with a mighty crash, bringing bottles and glasses smashing down on every side.

As the old salt got slowly to his feet and stamped red-faced into the pub, wondering how much the damage was going to cost him, the pensioners clapped and cheered: they might have lost their picnics, but it had been a day full of excitement!

Everyone's attention was centred on the pub, and Worzel Gummidge took advantage of the distraction caused by Saucy Nancy's escapade to creep into the luggage compartment and stow himself secretly away behind the empty picnic baskets, so that by the time Aunt Sally came to look for him he was nowhere to be seen.

Forlorn, she sat down on a bench overlooking the sea and began to cry.

There was a noise from the pub. The old salt emerged, even more red-faced and furious than when

he went in, wheeling his figurehead back to his ship.
As he passed Aunt Sally she went rigid and lifeless —
and not a moment too soon, for hard on the heels of
the old salt came Mr Peters and Mrs Braithwaite, leading the straggling pensioners back to the coach.

'Do you see what I see, Mr Peters?' asked the
farmer's wife, pulling up short at the bench. 'Now,
are you still going to tell me that that isn't Mr Shepherd's Aunt Sally?'

'But what's it doing *here*?'

'What was that gentleman's figurehead doing rolling down that hill?' she countered, 'and how can one
tramp eat twenty-five picnics? There's funny things
happen at the seaside, Mr Peters!' and motioning him
to take the shoulders, she picked up the Aunt Sally's
legs and lugged her over to the coach.

'Shall I put your sticks of rock in there as well?' she
asked, as Mr Peters stowed the Aunt Sally carefully
away in the luggage compartment.

'You might as well,' he agreed, 'only I hope this
really *is* Mr Shepherd's Aunt Sally, otherwise we *will*
be in trouble!'

The coach rolled lazily home through the countryside, dropping the pensioners one by one at their
homes as it passed through the village, and when only
the farmer and his wife were left, Mr Peters drove
down the narrow lane to Scatterbrook Farm, pulling
up outside the gate to the yard.

John and Sue ran out to meet them as they clambered down and stretched their legs.

'Did you have a nice time?' cried Sue.

Mrs Braithwaite chuckled. 'Well! Let's say an *eventful* time! Still, I think the old folk enjoyed it.'

'I could do with a cup of tea before I run over to Mr Shepherd's,' Mr Peters announced.

'Did you bring us any rock?' asked John as the adults made for the kitchen.

'Is that all you've been thinking about all day long? Go on, then, look in the boot!' laughed his father.

They ran round the coach and threw up the hatch of the luggage compartment. There, sound asleep, with a blissful smile and a lot of pink sticky mess on her face, lay Aunt Sally, clutching a half-eaten stick of rock.

'It's Aunt Sally,' cried Sue, 'and she's eaten all our rock!'

'Oh no she hasn't,' said John, pointing to where Worzel Gummidge lay just as sound asleep and just as messy, '*She* only ate half of it!'

'Oh, *Worzel*, what are we to do with you?' sighed Sue, as the scarecrow began to snore contentedly.

CHAPTER 2

A Lovesome Thing

A FARMER'S work is never done. It was the middle of summer; the corn was waving gently in the breeze, his cows chewed the cud under the shade of huge chestnut trees, his chickens pecked and clucked impatiently around the farmyard, and Mr Braithwaite had thought that, just for a change, he might have a nice lazy day sitting in a deckchair. But Dolly Braithwaite had other ideas: beside the house, just over the farmyard wall, there was a little kitchen garden and, she announced at breakfast, it was high time he did something about it, because the lawn was a foot high and the weeds were a disgrace. He grumbled and muttered for a while, but she got her way, and by the middle of the afternoon the garden was beginning to look almost tidy.

While her husband wrenched up the groundsel and the convolvulus, Mrs Braithwaite was out in the yard, talking to the Crowman.

'We've already got some thyme, in the herb garden,' she smiled. 'Leastways, Mr Crowman, I *think* we have!'

The Crowman's blue eyes twinkled behind his gold-rimmed glasses. He stood beside his ancient tricycle, whose wicker baskets were overflowing with neat little

43

bundles of fresh green herbs, and bright flowers wrapped in old newspapers.

'Ah,' he breathed softly, 'but this isn't your common-or-herb-garden thyme, Mrs Braithwaite. This is a bunch of wild thyme, with a rare flavour, that comes from the far meadow, close by Culvers Stream.'

Mr Peters ambled past, his hands in his pockets, and caught the Crowman's words. '"I know a bank where-on the wild thyme blows,"' he quoted.

Mrs Braithwaite looked quite surprised. 'Do you Mr Peters? You're picking up one or two country ways, then.'

He sighed. 'I don't mean *personally*, Mrs Braithwaite, it's *Shakespeare*! "I know a bank whereon the wild thyme blows and ... and ..." how *does* it go?' he frowned.

'It goes nicely with lemon,' murmured the Crowman persuasively. 'Thyme and lemon stuffing.'

Mrs Braithwaite was convinced. 'And that'll go nicely with the piece of lamb we're having on Sunday,' she said, accepting the little bundle gratefully. 'I'm much obliged to you, Mr Crowman.'

The Crowman smiled his strange, slow smile. 'A pleasure, Mrs Braithwaite.'

He turned his tricycle in the yard, calling over the wall to where the farmer was wheeling a barrow full of tools up the garden path. 'Good-day, Mr Braithwaite.'

The farmer gave him a cheery wave as he swung his leg over the saddle and pedalled serenely away.

'Jack, can I have a word with you?'

44

Mr Braithwaite, glad of any excuse to get away from gardening for a moment, put down his barrow and squeezed through the narrow little gate that led between the garden and the farmyard.

'It wasn't you that went off with my trug, was it?' went on his wife.

Mr Braithwaite frowned. 'Me? What would *I* do with your trug?'

'Well, I dunno! But *somebody* did. I put it down a minute ago and blow me down if it didn't disappear!'

The farmer turned and made his way back through the gate. 'Well, it wasn't me. I've got my own trug on top of the – Well blow me down!' he bellowed in surprise. 'It's gone! My wheelbarrow's gone! And all my tools with it!'

Worzel Gummidge crept along the lane, his boots kicking up little clouds of dust as he staggered under the weight of the wheelbarrow, loaded down with buckets and sickles and trowels and trugs. Spotting a slight gap in the hedge he suddenly turned off the lane, crashing the barrow ahead of him like a battering ram, and forced his way through the hedge into the field.

Coming along the lane an hour later Sue and John noticed the new gap in the hedge and promptly wriggled through it, full of curiosity, and caught sight of the scarecrow scrabbling away at a grassy bank a few yards away.

'Dang dratted pesky article,' he grumbled to himself as they crept up on him. 'I knows I left it somewhere's 'bout 'arvest time last year. If they dratted

squirrels 'ad it durin' the winter for nibblin' through
their 'ibernation I'll tan the tails off the varmints, dang
me if I don't!'

'What are you doing, Worzel?' asked Sue.

The scarecrow didn't look up. 'None o' your business,' he muttered rudely. 'Dang pesky little yewmans,
pokin' an' pryin'. Push off. Shoo.'

John sniffed. 'I don't care *what* he's doing. Come on,
Sue.'

'Thass it. You go an' bother some other yewmans,
an' leave an honest scarecrow in peace.'

'Have you lost something?' Sue inquired politely.
'We'll help you look for it if you'll tell us what it is.'

'Why for?' barked the scarecrow. 'So's you can keep
it if you finds it first?' He turned round for the first
time and tapped his forehead with a twiggy finger.
'I'm not as daft as I look, young madam. I'm not real
turnip in 'ere for nothing.'

'I wouldn't help him if he went down on his knees,'
decided John. 'Come *on.*'

''Ang on a minute. If I tells you what it is, do you
promise not to breathe it to a livin' soul? An' bring it
straight to me?' Sue nodded eagerly, bright-eyed, and
John gave a long-suffering sigh.

''Tis my special gardnin' 'ead. I 'id it last year. An'
now it's vanished.'

'A gardening head?' said John scornfully.

'Oo-ah! 'Tis a rare ol' 'ead for weedin' an' hoein' an'
plantin', so it is!'

'Are you going to do some weeding and hoeing and
planting, Worzel?' Sue asked, puzzled.

The scarecrow grinned. 'I'm goin' to get married, ain't I? Soon as Aunt Sally says as 'ow she's willin'. An' why ain't she said so up to now, d'you reckon?'

The children shook their heads, bewildered, quite unable to see where gardening and marriage fitted together.

The scarecrow snorted at them. 'I should'a thought that even a couple o' iggerant dumb-clucks like you'd know that. It's 'cos she's shamed o' me 'cos I works for yewmans. Standin' in the middle o' a field all day, all sorts o' weather, scrittin' an' scrattin', scarin' yewmans' crows offen yewmans' vegetaters. So I'm givin' up workin' for yewmans,' he went on. 'In future I'm makin' it a rule to work for scarecrows in general an' one scarecrow in partickerler.' He stood up straight and thumped his straw chest. 'Me!'

Without another word he got down on his knees and began scrabbling in the grassy bank, leaving the children staring at the back of his tatty old coat.

'Come on, Sue,' said John with a sigh. 'He's off on one of his mad ideas again. If we stay here we'll only end up getting involved, and if we get involved we'll only end up getting blamed for something, as per usual.' And they strolled away across the field towards the river.

The next day dawned just as hot, and Mr Braithwaite decided that it was time to do some watering. As the children tumbled noisily down the steps of the pretty caravan and raced away out of the yard, he plodded out of the kitchen with a bright new galvanized bucket and plonked it down to fill under the tap by the door.

'Keeping busy?' called Mr Peters, hearing the clatter.

Mr Braithwaite strolled round the corner of the caravan and found Mr Peters leaning out of the big bay window. 'I always am,' he sighed. 'If it's not the farm, it's the kitchen garden.'

He was struck with a sudden thought. '*You* weren't doing a bit of gardening yesterday, I don't suppose?'

Mr Peters laughed. 'That'll be the day! If there's one thing in the world I *can't* turn my hand to, it's gardening.'

'Only somebody walked off with my wheelbarrow.'

They could hear the splashing of water from the tap as they talked.

'Not guilty, your honour,' called Mr Peters, ducking back into the caravan and coming down the steps.

The farmer scratched his head. 'Don't make sense. I will find out who took it, though. There's been too many things going absent of late. You going out?' he asked, as Mr Peters pulled on his smart sports jacket.

'Only to stretch my legs. As far as the village.'

'If you see P.C. Parsons you might mention my wheelbarrow.'

'If I do,' he agreed, 'but I wasn't thinking of going as far as the police station.'

The farmer smiled. 'No, but you might bump into

him in the bar at The Crown,' he said with a broad wink.

Mr Peters grinned uncertainly and made his way to the gate.

As he went back to his bucket Mr Braithwaite called over his shoulder, 'Whoever took it won't put one over on me a second time. They seem to think I haven't got the sense to come in out of the wet. Well I'm jiggered!' he cried, finding the bright new bucket gone and a little lake spreading across the cobbled yard.

It wasn't long before the bucket was perched on top of a growing pile of spades and forks, bales of twine and balls of green string on the missing wheelbarrow. Leaning back against the barrow, Sue stared up into the topmost branches of an oak.

'What makes you think it might be up there anyway, Worzel?' she called.

A disembodied voice floated down from on high. 'It's the sort o' place a crafty squirrel might 'ide it. 'Ceptin' it ain't 'ere,' grumbled the scarecrow. 'Look out below!'

Sue leapt out of the way as, with a crashing and tearing sound, the scarecrow threw himself out of the tree and plummeted to earth, bouncing off branches and hitting the ground like a sack of potatoes. One of his arms came adrift in the mad plunge, and Sue kindly picked it up. 'Do you *always* come down from trees like that?' she asked.

'If you knows a quicker way, missy,' said the scarecrow, struggling to a sitting position with his back against the trunk of a tree, 'I'll be obliged to learn it. Pass us that arm.'

Sue handed it over and Worzel Gummidge pushed and pulled until it was back more or less in its usual place.

'I thought you kept all your spare heads in the barn?' she said curiously.

The scarecrow sniffed. 'Can't keep a gardnin' 'ead cooped up all hours in the dark. A gardnin' 'ead needs sun an' air. It needs to feel a speck or two o' rain. I should'a thought that were obvious, even to a daft-'ead yewman.'

Sue leaned back against the wheelbarrow and smoothed her smock down over her knees. 'If it wasn't for humans there wouldn't *be* scarecrows,' she observed.

'Scarecrows can do without yewmans, little miss clever clogs. Leastways, this scarecrow can. Soon as I lays twigs on that there dratted gardnin' 'ead, I'm goin' to be the fust ever scarecrow farmer. Oo-ah! I reckon I might axe a yewman to be the fust-ever yewman-scarecrow. You don't want the job, I suppose?' he asked hopefully.

'Not likely,' she cried, leaping up and tossing her head. Worzel Gummidge shrugged as she strolled away.

'Suit yoursel'. Plenty more yewmans where you comes from,' he called. 'You might think different when you 'ears what the wages is! Three crows' feathers a day an' all the straw as you can stuff up your sleeve!'

As Sue disappeared over the top of the hill the scarecrow turned to more pressing matters. 'Truss me up in a combine-'arvester!' he muttered. 'Danged if I knows *where* I 'id that dratted 'ead!'

In the kitchen of the farmhouse, Mrs Braithwaite watched glumly as Mrs Bloomsbury-Barton went to work with a will on one of the farmer's wife's famous sponge cakes. Mrs Bloomsbury-Barton had a habit of 'just dropping in' for a moment on her friends whenever she happened to be passing, and eating them out of house and home. And on top of that, Mrs Braithwaite was aghast at what Mrs Bloomsbury-Barton had just suggested.

'*Speak?*' she gasped. 'Me? Get up in front of the entire village, Mrs Bloomsbury-Barton?'

Mrs Bloomsbury-Barton waved away the objection with a toss of her hand. 'The briefest of perorations will suffice, Mrs ... er ...'

'Braithwaite.'

'Mrs Braithwaite. Just the teeniest of talks. Forty-five minutes at the very most.'

Mrs Braithwaite shook her head, completely bewildered by the idea of speaking to the Village Institute. 'But ... talk about *what*?'

'On any subject you might care to choose,' allowed Mrs Bloomsbury-Barton graciously.

'But I can't make speeches, Mrs Bloomsbury-Barton! I've never got up on my hind legs in front of an audience in my entire life!'

Mrs Bloomsbury-Barton ignored the objection and helped herself to another large slice of cake.

'It's *extremely* wicked of you, Mrs Braithmore, to

leave this sponge cake on the table! You know very well I'm on a *strict* diet.'

Mrs Braithwaite half rose and moved to take away the cake, but Mrs Bloomsbury-Barton grabbed it first. 'Too late!' she cried. 'The damage has been done! Besides, as soon as we've finished arranging your little talk tomorrow afternoon, I might just manage another teensy-weensy slice. Or have we already finished our arranging?'

'But ... it's such short notice!' she stuttered.

Mrs Bloomsbury-Barton looked stern. 'If you keep on raising objections, I shall begin to think you're trying to shirk your communal duty.'

'*Besiding* which,' insisted Mrs Braithwaite, 'what *could* I talk about?'

Mrs Bloomsbury-Barton threw her podgy arms wide. 'Anything! The world is your oyster. So to speak.'

Mrs Braithwaite squirmed uncomfortably. 'I don't know anything *about* oysters, Mrs Bloomsbury-Barton.'

'I was speaking ... *figuratively*,' said Mrs Bloomsbury-Barton in her most patronizing tone of voice. 'How about a little chat on petit-point?'

'I don't *do* petit-point,' said Mrs Braithwaite glumly.

Mrs Bloomsbury-Barton leaned forward confidentially. 'Neither do I!' she confessed, 'but I could jolly well soon sit down and jot down a few notes sufficient for a little talk on the subject.'

'Why don't you?' said Mrs Braithwaite quickly.

Mrs Bloomsbury-Barton sighed. 'I *would* Mrs Braithwold, were it not for the servants.'

Mrs Braithwaite looked baffled. 'Servants? Where do they come into it?'

'You cannot imagine how lucky you are not to have to keep both eyes firmly fixed on servants twenty-four hours of every day. I have a maid, a cook and a chauffeur, and gracious me, there are times when I'm quite sure I'd be better off fending for myself, so to speak. You don't keep servants, do you?' she asked suddenly.

Mrs Braithwaite shook her head at the very thought of it.

'Excellent!' beamed Mrs Bloomsbury-Barton. 'So there's nothing to stop you writing out your little talk, is there?'

'But what *about*?' moaned Mrs Braithwaite yet again.

Mrs Bloomsbury-Barton swivelled round to look at the little farmhouse kitchen, and spotted on the wide mantelpiece a pair of tiny Staffordshire figures and a huge Doulton jug. 'There!' she pointed, 'Why not talk about your little pieces of pottery? Staffordshire, aren't they?' She levered her fat hips out of the chair and waddled over to the mantelpiece to examine the jug. 'And isn't this Doulton ware?'

Mrs Braithwaite poopoohed the idea. 'They're only ornaments. They've been in the family ... oh, donkey's years. Those little figures belonged to my mother, and that old jug was her mother's before that.'

Mrs Bloomsbury-Barton put the jug down again and rubbed her hands with satisfaction. 'Fascinating!

That's all you need to say tomorrow afternoon. Just
... embellish it a little.' She took down the jug and
thrust it at Mrs Braithwaite. 'And you *must* bring it
along with you to illustrate your little talk. I'm sure
the entire audience will be agog, Mrs Braithstone.'

'Do you really think so, Mrs Bloomsbury-Barton?'
asked Mrs Braithwaite, still far from convinced.

'No other word for it, simply agog!' Mrs Bloomsbury-Barton assured her, helping herself to another
slice of sponge cake.

A few moments later, Mrs Bloomsbury-Barton was
at the door into the farmyard, booming her good-byes
to the apprehensive Mrs Braithwaite.

In the kitchen garden, where he was busy with a
hose and a lawn sprinkler, Mr Braithwaite ducked
behind a wall at the sound of her voice, and in the
caravan John slid down in the window seat and stayed
out of sight until her heavy footsteps passed and faded
away.

Soon the farmyard was silent again, and Mr Braithwaite straightened up. Having lost his bucket he'd laid
a length of hose from the tap by the kichen door and
stretched it to the middle of the lawn where a sprinkler
played, spraying the grass in slow circles. As he
watched, the sprinkler went slower, and slower, and
finally stopped altogether.

He slipped through the little gate and set off across
the yard. 'Whoever's messing about with that tap,' he
called, 'can just turn it on again, this minute. Else
they'll know about it!' he finished angrily, going back
to the kitchen garden again.

Slamming the gate to behind him he stopped in his tracks and stared open-mouthed at the lawn. 'Well, I'm flummoxed!' he muttered, for where the sprinkler had been there was now nothing but a small circle of damp, flattened grass. The farmer picked up the hose pipe.

In the yard, as if obeying his orders, an unseen hand turned the tap on again.

A gush of water shot out of the hose.

Mr Braithwaite jumped back, drenched, and cursed furiously as he ran back to the tap.

But there was not a soul to be seen...

As soon as Mrs Bloomsbury-Barton was out of sight, John ambled out of the caravan and set off up the lane with his hands in his pockets, whistling tunelessly. A great tit chattered angrily at him from a blackthorn, and clouds of midges danced over the almost-dry bed of the stream.

Balancing on the topmost rung of the stile, the boy stared across Ten-acre Field, but Worzel Gummidge was nowhere to be seen, so he carried on down the lane away from the farm. Just before he reached the turning to the village, he glanced through a gap in the hedge and pulled up with a start.

'Crikey Moses!' he whispered, creeping through on his hands and knees. For there, at the edge of the turnip field, sat Worzel Gummidge, pulling up turnips, examining them, and tossing them one by one over his shoulder into the hedge.

''Op it,' he barked, catching sight of the boy.

'What *are* you doing?'

'I won't tell 'ee again. Buzz off.'

'If Farmer Braithwaite catches you he'll go off his *rocker*,' cried John as the scarecrow discarded another turnip.

'Dang titchy yewmans worritin' scarecrows. Orter be a scarecrow law against it, so there should.' He up-rooted another turnip and examined it closely, turning it this way and that. 'An' that ain't the one as I'm lookin' for neither, tarnation take the pesky thing!'

'But what *are* you looking for?'

Worzel Gummidge glanced up irritably and hurled a turnip at him. 'Don't yewman 'eads take in nothin'?' he yelled. 'Or ain't that your rememberin' 'ead as you're wearing'? I'm lookin' for my gardnin' 'ead, same as what I told you more nor once. I reckons as 'ow I might'a buried it 'ere.'

'In a *turnip* field?' asked John incredulously.

'Why not? 'Tis a turnip, bain't it?' observed the scarecrow with an air of sweet reason. 'Do you want to 'elp me look for 'un?'

John imagined what Mr Braithwaite's reaction would be if he caught him grubbing up half-grown turnips. 'Not likely! Not here!'

'Why for not?'

'Looking for a turnip in a turnip field? You'd stand more chance looking for a needle in a haystack!' cried the boy, scampering away.

The scarecrow's eyes lit up. 'A what? What did 'e say? A what-fot in a where-for? A 'aystack! That wor it! Now I remembers where I put that there 'ead!'

He frowned. 'But 'oo told that titchy yewman where it were, eh?'

Shaking his head, he levered himself to his feet and lurched erratically towards the gap in the hedge, diving in head first and dragging himself through to the lane. 'Dang dratted leg!' he shouted when he tried to stand up and found that he'd left a leg behind in a thornbush. 'More trouble nor it's worth!'

He hopped back to the hedge and tugged it free, leaving shreds of straw waving in the wind. 'It'd serve 'ee right, leg, if I was to leave 'ee off completely an' go round on t'other leg, 'oppin' everywhere!'

A lean black figure strolled out of the woods by the river at Foggy Bottom and sniffed the air with satisfaction. A light breeze ruffled the Crowman's long black frock-coat, and touched the strands of white hair that strayed out from beneath his tall hat. In his arms there were bundles of flowers, and herbs fresh from the river bank.

He strolled through the lush green fields, nodding greetings to nesting birds, then spotted a commotion in a haystack and stopped with a smile on his lips.

As he watched, a bale of hay detached itself and tumbled down, closely followed by the scarecrow, arms and legs waving as he rolled to the ground.

'Dang me!' he yelled, clambering to his feet and examining a bundle wrapped in potato sacking, 'if that there titchy yewman weren't right after all! 'Tis 'ere! My gardnin' 'ead! Arter all this time. By swedes an' turnips, but there'll be some rare ol' plantin' an' sowin' an' weedin' an' hoein' goin' on now all right!'

The Crowman shook his head as he watched the scarecrow scampering away with his bundle. A slow smile played around the corners of his mouth, and there was a far-away look in his eyes, as though he were thinking of things that had been, or were yet to be.

'More trouble, Worzel?' he whispered to himself. 'Whenever you acquire a spare head it always seems to work out that two heads are more trouble than one.'

The very next day, as if the weather itself knew that the scarecrow had found his gardening head, it rained.

The children awoke to a downpour, and moped and moaned around the caravan all morning until John spotted the bedraggled figure of Worzel Gummidge peering out round a corner of the garage at Scatter-brook Farm. He and his sister dashed across the road and joined the scarecrow staring glumly at the rain.

'You aren't going to get much gardening done today, Worzel,' said Sue sympathetically.

The scarecrow clutched the sacking bundle that contained his head and sighed. ''Tain't fair, so 'tain't! 'Tain't fair at all!'

'Of course it isn't fair!' said John in a feeble attempt at a joke. 'It's raining.'

The scarecrow ignored him. 'I've a good mind to 'ave a right ol' sulk, so I 'ave, an' that would serve this weather right. Look out there. I've 'ad this 'ere gar-dnin' 'ead a 'ole day now, an' all the weather's done is chuck it down with rain. I axe you, what's the good of 'avin' a gardnin' 'ead when the weather bain't on your side?'

He put down his sacking-wrapped head on a bench at the end of the garage and shook his fist at the clouds that hung over the farm.

'You could go out and plant some rice,' suggested John sarcastically.

The scarecrow scowled at him. 'Don't talk daft! 'Ow could I go outdoors, in weather like this, with a gardnin' 'ead on my shoulders? It'd only need a drop o' rain on it, would an agricultural 'ead like that, an' it'd start to sprout. Don't suit nobody, don't weather like this, an' that's a fact.'

John was determined to be funny. 'Yes it does,' he argued. 'It suits the ducks.'

'Stop *teasing* him, John,' insisted Sue. 'You'll only make him ... you *have*!' she cried, as the scarecrow stiffened, his arms outstretched. 'He's going to sulk!'

While the children stared out at the rain from the garage Mr Braithwaite, looking just as miserable, stared out at it from the kitchen, his shoulders hunched and his hands thrust deep in his trouser pockets. He glanced at the big old clock on the dresser.

'Hey up, missus,' he called over his shoulder, 'are you anywhere near ready yet?'

'Shan't be much more than a minute,' his wife's voice floated down the stairs.

He chuckled good-naturedly, 'We haven't got much more nor a minute neither! I hope you know we're going to be late!'

'Oh, Jack!' she fluttered as she came into the kitchen, pulling on her coat. 'I do wish I wasn't going! Do we have to?'

'Course *you've* got to go. *You* promised. I'm only going along to give you moral support. It was you what let that Bloomsbury-Barton woman talk you into it.'

'Only 'cos she was so *persistent*,' complained Mrs Braithwaite, checking her make-up in a little pocket mirror, 'I wish I hadn't, I do really. I never made a speech in all my life before. Now where's my hat?' she wondered.

'You're wearing it,' he answered softly.

'Oh so I am. Now, bring that jug,' she ordered.

Her husband took the huge jug down from the mantelpiece and turned it round in his big horny hands. 'What do you want this old thing for?' he asked.

'I *told* you! I've got to talk about it, haven't I? Now go and wrap it up. I'll meet you by the car.'

With the jug under his arm and his collar up against the rain, Mr Braithwaite galloped across the yard and shot into the garage.

'Hello, you two?' he said in surprise, 'Ready already? Well, you'll just have to hang on a minute while I wrap this up,' and grabbing an old sack he carefully wrapped the jug and laid it on the work-bench.

'Now then –' he began, then stopped and stared as he caught sight of the scarecrow for the first time. 'What on earth is *that* doing in here?' he asked as Mrs Braithwaite followed him into the garage.

The children looked at one another nervously.

'Er ... I brought it in here, Mr Braithwaite,' said John.

The farmer looked baffled. 'You did, lad? What on earth for?'

John thought furiously. 'It was raining hard,' he decided. 'I didn't think you'd want it to get wet.'

Mr Braithwaite looked disbelieving, then amazed, and finally burst out in a great deep-throated guffaw of laughter as he turned to his wife.

'Well!' he cried, 'I've heard of some things in my days, but bringing in a scarecrow out of the wet! That takes the cake does that, it really does! Come on the pair of you, get in the car!'

He held the door open to let the children into the back seat, helped his wife into the passenger seat, and was about to get in himself when she called out to him, 'Jack! The *jug*! Honestly,' she went on as he collected a sacking-wrapped bundle from the work-bench, 'you'd forget your head if it wasn't fastened on, wouldn't you?'

He chuckled at the thought, and gave her the parcel as he got in and started the car. In the back, the children's mouths gaped in horror.

'Sue! That's Worzel's ...'

'Ssssh!' whispered Sue, and with a shrug to one another, as if to say, 'There's nothing *we* can do about it anyway', they sat back to watch the rainy landscape roll past.

In the garage, as the car drew away and disappeared down the lane, Worzel Gummidge came to life with a face as dark and thundery as the weather itself. He shook his fist after the car.

'Never mind 'im forgettin' '*is* 'ead, missus!' he bellowed into the rain. 'Thass my 'ead you's gone off with!' He lurched over to the work-bench and unwrapped the parcel left behind by Mr Braithwaite.

'A jug? A pesky ol' jug for a gardnin' 'ead? That ain't no fair swaps at all, so it ain't!' A gleam came into the scarecrow's eye.

'Oo-ah!' he whispered to himself. 'You was takin' this 'ere jug down that Institute place, wasn't you? My little robin redbreast told me that, so 'e did. Makin' a speech an' all, so you be. Well, missus, two can play at that game. You'm not the only one as can stand up in public an' say a word or three! I'll show 'ee!' And with that Worzel Gummidge stamped out of the garage and crossed the yard to the barn where, hidden away in a cider barrel he found a battered old black Gladstone bag and pulled out from inside it a weird-looking, mouldering, grey-green head, with a laurel wreath wound round the brow and a cracked, gold-rimmed, half-frame pince-nez perched on the end of its drooping nose.

'Oo-ah!' he grunted happily, sitting on a bale of hay and setting the head carefully on his lap. 'My speechifyin' 'ead! I 'ope it still works. Ain't 'ad no call to use it for a year or four, 'appen a 'ole fortnight. 'Ere goes!' and he hauled and screwed and wrenched his workaday head loose, ramming and wriggling and squashing the speechifying head down in its place. He smacked his lips experimentally and coughed to clear his throat.

'Speak the speech I pray as I pronounced it to you,' he began mellifluously. 'Trippingly on the tongue –

ooh it's as good as new!' and he leapt to his feet and headed out into the rain.

Outside the village hall, just as the rain finally eased off and a pale sun broke through the clouds, Mr Braithwaite stood chatting with Mr Peters while his wife prepared herself for her speech. 'Not coming inside to see the fun, Mr Peters?' he asked.

'Can't,' replied the other, indicating a ladder propped up against the wall. 'I've got this window to fix. And then I've got to go and take a look at Mr Shepherd's coal-house door.'

The farmer chuckled and shook his head. 'For someone who's out of work you're the busiest man I know!'

'How's Mrs Braithwaite feeling?' asked Mr Peters. 'Nervous, is she?'

'Nervous? Noooo, she ain't nervous! Nervous ain't the word! She's *petrified*! She wishes it were anybody doing it but her,' her husband laughed, and wandered into the hall to take his seat at the back of the audience.

Behind the stage, in a little ante-room, the farmer's wife *was* petrified. Mrs Bloomsbury-Barton was brandishing her very best smelling-salts under her nose, and they were doing no good at all.

'Pull yourself together, Mrs Braithwaite!' she commanded sternly. 'You are going out on that stage to address a few friends, that is all!'

'I couldn't feel no worse, Mrs Bloomsbury-Barton,

if I was going out to face a firing squad. And that's the truth,' moaned Dolly Braithwaite unhappily.

'I'm sure if you stood up and went across to the window for a breath of fresh air –'

'I *can't* stand up!'

'Such nonsense –'

'I *can't*,' she insisted. 'My legs are turned to jelly and my feet have got the collywobbles.'

'You really *must* pull yourself together! Or some sort of action must be taken. Even if it means my going out and delivering your little talk myself.'

A ray of hope dawned in Mrs Braithwaite's eyes as Mrs Bloomsbury-Barton's words gave her an idea. She began to moan even more pitifully.

Outside the hall, as Mr Peters climbed his ladder and examined the window, the scarecrow crouched behind the hedge, watching with narrowed eyes and muttering to himself, 'I would say to the house as I would say to those who have joined this government that I have nothing to offer but blood, toil, tears and turnips, oo-ah, but if we stands by an' lets yewmans steal scarecrows' 'eads no scarecrow's ever goin' to be able to call 'is 'ead 'is own. 'Ear, 'ear, Bravo!'

Mrs Bloomsbury-Barton strode imperiously out on to the little stage of the village hall just as the audience was getting restless and starting to mutter about its tea.

'Dear friends!' she called, and slowly silence descended over the room. 'Dear friends. Some sad news first,' she beamed. 'Mrs Dolly Braithwaite has suddenly been taken unwell and is unable to appear. However,' she went on as a murmur of sympathy ran through the audience, 'it is nothing serious, I am happy to say. But I hear you saying to yourselves, what's to become of the lecture? Are we to be disappointed? The short answer is, no! For someone has very kindly offered to step into the breach.' She paused for dramatic effect. 'Yes, you've guessed it, *me*!' she cried, and waited for applause, but none came.

Instead the audience, who'd heard more than enough of Mrs Bloomsbury-Barton in the past, began to shuffle and look decidedly irritable. Quite unaware of this, Mrs Bloomsbury-Barton ground on. 'It was Mrs Braithwaite's intention to talk to you this afternoon about the various quaint ornaments and common-or-garden knick-knacks to be found in *ordinary* people's homes. Well, I think I can safely say that I have visited sufficient *ordinary* homes to be well qualified to speak to you on Mrs Braithwaite's chosen subject. My little talk this afternoon, therefore, is called Working Class Paraphernalia. Now then, are we all sitting comfortably?' she asked, and as the depressed audience sank lower and lower in its chairs she launched upon her monologue.

If Worzel Gummidge had stopped his own speechifying for a moment, he would have heard Mrs Bloomsbury-Barton's booming voice from well outside the hall, but he was enjoying the sound of his own voice far too much to listen to anybody else. 'I see you stand like turnips in a field,' he declared, clambering up the ladder while Mr Peters was away looking for a pane of glass and some fresh putty. 'Strainin' upon the start the game's afoot follow this spirit and upon this charge cry up with Worzel, the Crowman an' Saint Jarge, oo-ah!' and he peered in through the broken window to see Mrs Bloomsbury-Barton in full spate.

'It is not necessary for me to tell you,' she told them, 'that I am not referring to the kind of *genuine* antiques such as one might come across in the residences of the *upper* classes and the aristocracy – those little collectors' pieces that grace my own drawing-room. No, dear friends,' she gushed, in her very snootiest tones, 'I am talking to you this afternoon only about such items as can be picked up cheaply in dusty secondhand shops or on common market-traders' stalls –' she suddenly looked up, broke off, turned white, gave a little shriek, and collapsed in a heap on the stage.

There was uproar in the hall. Three of the strongest men in the room managed to drag her to her feet and get her into a chair; someone was dispatched to the ante-room to fetch her smelling-salts; and Sue and John giggled together as a dozen people flapped and flustered round her.

'I'm terribly sorry,' she gasped eventually. 'Please excuse me. I just had the *most* frightening experience. Just for a moment – I suppose it could have been a trick of the light, but just for a moment it seemed as if I could see the most evil-looking face I've ever seen in my life. Peering in at the window there. Like some awful ghastly being from another world.'

Everyone turned to stare at the window, only to find that the scarecrow had slipped away and been replaced by Mr Peters, busily puttying the pane of glass.

He waved.

The audience waved back.

Some cheered.

Others giggled.

Mrs Bloomsbury-Barton recovered her composure and looked rather huffy.

'Turn back this way, please!' she snapped. 'I am sufficiently recovered to continue with the talk. Bric-à-brac found in ordinary homes. I would like to point out, although it is the exception rather than the rule, that occasionally one comes across an exciting find that may prove to be quite valuable. This happened to me only yesterday, and I have brought along my little discovery to show you –'

She beckoned to Sue, sitting in the front row, and picked up the sacking-wrapped parcel.

With a terrible feeling of foreboding the girl moved slowly forwards. 'But I am not going to stand here on the stage and hold it up for all of you to see. Oh no! I am going to ask you to pass it round among yourselves so that you may feel the texture and examine the colour. Little girl, hand this down to the front row for me!' she commanded, passing the parcel to Sue.

'But ... but Mrs Bloomsbury-Barton!'

'Do as you are told, little girl!' she insisted, and as the turnip was unwrapped and solemnly passed down the row she went rambling on with her speech. 'Of course, as you can see, the piece you are looking at could not, under the circumstances, be described as priceless –'

A farmer poked and sniffed the turnip, and nodded his agreement.

'Nevertheless, it is, as I'm sure you must all agree, a rare and attractive *objet d'art*.'

Three ladies from the Young Wives giggled together as they tried to imagine it in an art gallery.

'And I know that each and every one of you would be delighted to have one of your very own to grace your own mantelpiece or sideboard –'

As the turnip travelled along a second row and then a third the audience began to shudder and shake with suppressed laughter.

Mrs Bloomsbury-Barton frowned, but pressed on determinedly. 'There are some of you, I dare suppose, who might even have such a beautiful piece as this tucked away in a drawer or cupboard or concealed in a trunk in the attic, without realizing what a treasure you are hiding from the world. Well, to such persons I can only say –'

The suppressed laughter began to bubble over as the turnip made its way back to the front of the hall, row by row, passing from hand to hand.

'What's going on?' hissed Mrs Bloomsbury-Barton to Sue, who could barely control her own giggles.

'Please, Mrs Bloomsbury-Barton, it's a turnip!'

'What is?'

'What they're looking at.'

'Nonsense, girl! It's a perfect example of a nineteenth century –' her voice faded away and her jaw dropped as the turnip arrived at the front row again.

Sue solemnly handed it up to her, and there was a brief moment of silence as the hall watched her staring open-mouthed at the grubby, muddy vegetable.

'My lords, ladies an' gentlemen,' came a rich, deep voice from the back of the hall as Worzel Gummidge, his speechifyin' 'ead in good working order, marched in, bowing right and left as he spoke. 'Friends, Romans an' countrymen lend me your ears I come to tell 'ee that the pound in your pocket is better than the wind of change you know it makes sense, oo-ah, an' furthermore if me right honourable colleague on t'other side o' the chamber don't 'and over my gardnin' 'ead she'll be well an' truly sorry 'cos I can stand 'ere blatherin' a whole lot longer than what she can, so 'ow about it missus?' he finished, striding up on to the platform and sweeping the turnip from her grasp.

He examined it for blemishes and strode back again down the hall, still speechifying. 'Alas, poor Yorick, I knew 'im 'Oratio a fellow of infinite jest, oo-ah! an' in conclusion I would just say this up with me an' down with everybody else!'

At the door he paused, bowed low, and swept out to a furious round of applause, while Mrs Bloomsbury-Barton slowly fainted to the floor.

A mile away, in the lane, when he was almost at the stile that led into Ten-acre Field, Worzel Gummidge was still speechifying as he knocked the mud from his gardening head.

'Where be your gibes now? Your gambols? Your songs? Your flashes of merriment as were wont to set the table on a roar?'

He stopped dead and bowed low, more nervously than he had in the hall. 'Arternoon, your 'ighness.'

'More heads, Worzel?' asked the Crowman softly. He was sitting on the stile, patient as an oak tree, as if he'd known that the scarecrow was coming and had decided that this would be a good place to wait for him. 'More mischief?'

The scarecrow shook his head indignantly. 'Oh no, your mightiness. I only been gettin' back my gardnin' 'ead you very kindly once 'orticultured on my behalf.'

The Crowman nodded and jumped lightly down from the stile. 'I'm glad to hear it. Because now that you've managed to retrieve it, Worzel, you can set it to a purpose. I've got some work for you to do.'

The scarecrow beamed. '*Work*, your majesty?'

'*Work,* Worzel. Follow me,' said the Crowman, climbing aboard his tricycle and setting off very slowly down the lane.

The next morning, very early, when the dew was still wet upon the grass and there was a breathless quiet in the air, the children woke early, dressed, and set off without a word, following paths they'd never seen before as though they were being led along them, deep into the woods at the foot of the hills to the thick hedge round the garden of the Crowman's house.

There they shook themselves, as animals do when they wake, and looked around to see the scarecrow's head and shoulders over the hedge. They could just make out that he was sprawled out in a deckchair, making the most of the early morning sun.

'Hello, Worzel,' they called happily. 'Why aren't you in Ten-acre Field?'

'Oo-ah. Doin' a bit o' gardnin' for the Crowman, so I am,' he replied proudly.

'*Gardening?*' asked Sue incredulously.

'Thass right. Mowin' this 'ere lawn for 'im, ain't I?'

John sneered, 'Sitting in a deckchair?'

'Oo-ah! Ain't nothin' like a gardnin' 'ead for findin' a means o' doin' a bit o' agriculture the easy way.'

The children ran up to the hedge and stood on tiptoe to peer over. There, dotted all over the lush grass of the Crowman's lawn, were dozens and dozens of rabbits, nibbling busily away at the grass.

'Thass the way, me little beauties,' encouraged the scarecrow. 'We'll soon 'ave this 'ere lawn trimmed juss the way the Crowman wants it.'

He glowered at the children. 'An' you shove off, you titchy yewmans. I'm too busy to chit-chat with the likes of you.'

As the children began to move disconsolately back the way they'd come, the scarecrow's voice drifted over the hedge and followed them, wheedling now. 'Oy! If you ain't got nothing better to do you might 'ave a scout round an' see if you can lay your 'ands on a bottle o' ginger beer an' a slice o' cake or two. An' it's thirsty work an' all, so it is. Oo-ah!'

The children smiled happily at one another.

'Up the workers!' muttered John.

'Too true,' his sister agreed as they strolled out through the woods towards the rolling hills.

CHAPTER 3
A Fair Old Pullover

ONE Saturday towards the end of summer, when young hedge-sparrows screamed from their nests, demanding even more food from their already exhausted parents, and the early morning air seemed heavy with heat even though the sun was still low in the sky, John and Sue made their way to Ten-acre Field to visit Worzel Gummidge and tell him that they were going shopping in the near-by market town with Mr Braithwaite and his wife. They could see from the stile that the scarecrow wasn't on his pole, but they wandered over to have a look at it just the same, and found his hat lying among the thick grass.

'You don't suppose he's *underneath* it, do you?' suggested Sue, rather dubiously.

'What do you mean, underneath?'

'You know. Sort of, *buried*. Up to the top of his head.'

John looked scornful. 'Course not, stupid.'

'He *could* be,' his sister insisted. 'He does get up to some funny tricks.'

'Pick it up and see.'

Sue shook her head. 'I don't like to. You pick it up.'

Hiding his nervousness, John stooped down and grabbed the hat, relieved to find nothing underneath it. 'There,' he said triumphantly. 'What did I tell you?'

Sue looked around Ten-acre Field, half-relieved and half-sorry. 'I wonder where he's gone to?' she mused. 'And why did he leave his hat behind?'

John lost interest in the scarecrow and turned away to head back to the stile.

'Dunno,' he called, 'Don't much care. Come on!' and he began to turn cartwheels on the thick grass, kicking up clouds of pollen from the clover.

In the farmyard, while Mr Braithwaite was busy trying to start the car ready for their expedition, Mrs Braithwaite was deep in conversation with the Crow-man.

'There's a dozen new-laid eggs in there,' she said solicitously, handing the tall, black-clothed figure a bulging brown paper bag with string handles, 'so don't you go breaking them.'

The Crowman tipped his hat courteously, took the bag from her and laid it gently in the front basket of his ancient tricycle.

'I won't,' he said softly. 'And I'm most deeply obliged to you, Mrs Braithwaite.'

The farmer's wife shook her head, making her plump cheeks wobble. 'Not half as much as I'm obliged to you. If you hadn't given me that bottle of jollop for them hens, I reckon we'd have lost at least half of them. Even the vet was flummoxed.' From the pocket of her striped apron she pulled out a tiny green glass bottle, oddly shaped, corked with a ground glass stopper, and peered closely at it as she spoke, 'He was wondering what this stuff was.'

The Crowman gave a deep chuckle, and his eyes seemed to be looking even further away than usual. 'An old countryman's remedy, Mrs Braithwaite. A sworn secret I once had passed on to me by a fell shepherd. He'd had it handed down to him by an Irish tinker of leprechaun descent,' he finished, deftly relieving her of the bottle and slipping it into one of the long pockets in the tails of his black frock-coat.

Mrs Braithwaite was suitably impressed. 'Well now, fancy that! Oh, and there's a fresh-pulled caulie in that bag as well. And a pound of my best dairy butter.'

The Crowman bowed. 'My most courteous thanks to you again, ma'am,' he murmured graciously, as he slipped on his trouser-clips.

'Mind how you go with them eggs now!'

'I will,' he assured her, wheeling his trike out of the yard.

Back in the kitchen, the farmer's wife suddenly stopped as a thought struck her. 'An Irish tinker of *leprechaun* descent?' she muttered with a frown. She shook her head and made her way upstairs.

'I'll sell you, m'girl!' bellowed Mr Braithwaite.

Outside the garage, his little car stood stubborn as a mule, refusing even to start. The farmer climbed out of the driving seat and walked round to open the bonnet, muttering under his breath, 'One o' these fine days I'll get me a new model, darn well see if I don't!'

Coming slowly out of the yard, the Crowman

stopped beside the car and touched his hat in a greeting.

'Or acquire an alternative means of transport,' he suggested gently.

The farmer straightened up and glanced at the big black tricycle. 'One like yours, eh?' he nodded, smiling. 'I reckon they might catch on, what with the price of petrol. Only I don't reckon I've got the leg-muscle for one o' them contraptions.'

The Crowman glanced at the oily engine under the open bonnet and fished in his pocket for the green glass bottle. 'In which predicament, Mr Braithwaite, might I suggest you try three drops of this in your carburettor?'

The farmer took the curious little bottle and held it up to the light.

'What the hummers is this?' he asked good-naturedly.

The Crowman leaned closer to him and spoke conspiratorially. 'An old mechanical lubrication,' he whispered. 'A sworn secret formula I had passed on to me by a Cornish knife-grinder, who'd had it handed down to him by the grandfather of the grandfather of the man who invented the spinning jenny.'

Mr Braithwaite's eyes lit up. His eyebrows rose. 'Well then!' he breathed, quite unable to think of anything more suitable to say. The Crowman nodded intently. 'I'll have the bottle back the next time I see you,' he said, touching his hat, climbing onto his tricycle and pedalling slowly away.

The farmer watched him go, a frown deepening on

his face. He slapped his hat on the car's roof-rack, growling to himself, with the expression of a man who thinks he's just been taken for a ride.

' "Grandfather of the grandfather of the man what invented the spinning-jenny." He must think I'm half sharp!' he grumbled, but when he bent his head to the engine he let three drops of clear liquid from the tiny bottle drip into the carburettor, just in case . . .

While Mr Braithwaite was engrossed in his engine's innards, there was a rustling from behind the car and a pair of beady eyes peered over the wall, followed by a twiggy hand on the end of a broomhandle arm that shot out like lightning, grabbed the farmer's best tweed hat from the roof-rack of the car, and shot back again.

Mr Braithwaite straightened up, still muttering to himself, and made his way round to the driver's seat. The engine started first pull, and with a little chuckle of delight he got out and set off to collect Dolly, reaching out for his hat as he went.

He frowned, and looked around.

Harry, the farm labourer, was passing.

'Harry? Have you seen my hat?'

'Your 'at?'

'My best *tweedy* hat,' said Mr Braithwaite irritably. 'I left it atop the car. You haven't been playing silly beggars with it, have you?'

'Of course I haven't,' said Harry indignantly. 'I *wouldn't*, Mr Braithwaite.'

The angry farmer stamped away across the dusty cobbles of the farmyard and headed for the kitchen door, 'Dolly,' he yelled as he kicked off his boots and went in. 'You about?'

'Coming, Jack,' she called, following her words into the room. She had her coat on, and was setting her scarf about her head, preparatory to knotting it.

'You haven't set eyes, I don't suppose, on my hat?' asked her husband petulantly.

'Your hat?' she replied in surprise. 'Your tweed hat?'

He nodded. 'Your *best* tweed hat?'

He nodded again. 'Why, I'm sure I saw you, not five minutes since, crossing the farmyard with it on your head!'

The farmer scratched his bald patch, 'It ain't there now, though, is it? Pop upstairs for me, would you, and see if it's on the bed?'

She sighed a long-suffering sigh, took off her scarf and laid it on the table by the window, and was about to set off up the steep staircase when she noticed the tiny green glass bottle in her husband's hands, and frowned.

'What *are* you doing with that?' she asked in surprise. 'The hens haven't got colic again already, have they?'

He looked down at the bottle and shook his head. 'Does this,' he said patiently, '*look* like a potion for your colicky hens?'

'Doesn't matter what it *looks* like,' said Dolly stubbornly, 'I'm saying what it *is*. A potion for colicky hens, handed down by an Irish tinker of leprechaun extraction.'

Mr Braithwaite laughed, 'Don't talk daft, woman!

It's a carburettor lubricant is this. Passed on by the grandfather of the grandfather of the man what invented the spinning-jenny. Now are you going to have a look for my tweedy hat or aren't you?'

As Dolly Braithwaite made her way upstairs the farmer stood in the doorway of the kitchen, staring out over the farmyard and breathing in deep lungfuls of the smell of dung. The children scampered in through the field-gate by the caravan and waved happily to him.

'Are you two ready?' he called, 'because we'll be away in a minute.'

'Ready in a tick!' cried Sue.

'You don't mean your car's actually *going*, do you?' said John as they disappeared into the caravan to change.

'Cheeky monkey!' laughed the farmer, turning back into the kitchen just a moment too late to see his wife's scarf whisking its way out of the window in the grip of a set of twiggy fingers.

'This is all I could find,' she said, coming back down the stairs and tossing her husband a corduroy cap. 'You'll have to wear that.'

She looked at the table by the window and frowned. 'You haven't moved my scarf, I don't suppose?'

'What would I be doing moving your scarf?' he chaffed.

'Well. *Somebody* has.'

'You're always losing something,' he joked, taking her arm and leading her out to the car. 'You'd lose your head if it wasn't fastened on.'

She stood back at the open door of the car to let the

children in. 'It'd be a blessing to *you* to lose your head! You're already lost your hat!'

Round the corner of the garage Harry appeared, peering at the ground, his head snaking from side to side like a sniffing bloodhound.

'You lost something, Harry?' asked the farmer.

'Yes, Mr Braithwaite, I have,' he answered mournfully. 'My gloves. I only put 'em down for a moment while I blew me nose, and the next thing I knew, there they were, gone. I don't suppose *you've* any idea where they've gone?'

Mr Braithwaite shook his head. 'Same place as my hat and her scarf, I dare say. Anyway, let's get off out of here before we lose the wheels off the car!' he said, pulling away.

Crows watched incuriously from the tops of tall elms as the little car pottered out of the farmyard and down the lane. Rabbits froze in the long grass of the verges until they'd passed. On the outskirts of the village, where they turned away towards a wider road that wound along the valley to the market town, a mare and her foal stared over a five-barred gate, nodding in a friendly way and tossing their heads to rid themselves of flies. Clouds of dust had followed the car along the lane, but on the tarmac of the main road the tyres hummed, singing little songs on the hot surface.

Slowing down to turn a corner, Mr Braithwaite frowned as he caught sight of a couple of cyclists going in the opposite direction, laughing uproariously and pointing at the car.

'What's the matter with them?' he wondered out loud.

'It's this old car, I expect,' answered his wife. 'I've been telling you for long enough to get a new one.'

They drove on in silence, enjoying the rich, varied greens of the countryside, hedges and fields and trees and crops in a hundred different colours, yet all of them somehow still green. Yellow-hammers chattered at them from telegraph wires, and high overhead a kestrel hung on the wind with quivering wings.

At the edge of a village, near another farm very like his own, Mr Braithwaite spotted a herd of cows being driven into a meadow by a farm labourer, and slowed down to cast a professional eye over them. Goggle-eyed with astonishment, the labourer forgot all about his cows and stood stock-still, staring at the car. Left to themselves, the cows milled about all over the road, and Mr Braithwaite had to stop the car.

'Hoy!' he called, winding down the window. 'Look what you're doing! You're not fit to be in charge of that herd on a public highway!' and shaking his head at the incompetence of other people's cowmen, he drove very carefully through the herd and away.

A cow pressed against the open-mouthed farm labourer. He took a pace back to steady himself, and slid very slowly and gently down into a half-full ditch.

'I'm fed up with people laughing at this car,' grumbled Mr Braithwaite. 'It's not as if it's *that* old.'

'They wouldn't laugh if you got a nice new, shiny, *posh* car,' his wife suggested.

'Yes, well, if I had a lot of nice, new, shiny posh money...'

They came to a crossroads and slowed down to turn left into the market town. Coming towards them on his bicycle a policeman wobbled precariously as he spotted the car, clutched wildly at his helmet, and rode straight into a signpost.

'What on earth's wrong with him?' asked the exasperated farmer.

'I think a nice blue car next time,' mused his wife, miles away in her own dreams. 'It'll go with my scarf. If it ever turns up.'

'I dunno. Anyone'd think we'd got an ostrich on the roof, the way people are looking.

But an ostrich on the roof wouldn't have attracted half as much attention as Worzel Gummidge did!

Having heard about the trip into town from his little robin redbreast, he'd decided to hitch a lift, and had slipped onto the roof-rack when no one was looking. All the way along he'd enjoyed himself hugely, a great grin splitting his turnip face as the wind whistled through his straw.

Crammed down over his head was Mr Braithwaite's missing hat, and to keep out the cold the scarecrow wore Harry's gloves on his twiggy fingers and Mrs Braithwaite's scarf round his broomhandle neck. From the roof he waved to passing sheep and shook his fist at crows and rooks. Sometimes he stood up with his arms outstretched in the proper scarecrow position and sometimes, just for a change, he sat down, cross-legged, with his arms folded across his chest like a genie on a magic carpet.

'Oo-ah!' he speculated, as they came to the outskirts of the town. 'That cow-yewman what fell in the ditch were good, but I reckons that dang policeman were better. On t'other 'and, the cow-yewman got wet, so 'e did. Ar.'

His brow furrowed as he tried to decide which spectacle had been more fun, and he concentrated so hard that he woke with a start when the car pulled into the car park in the town centre.

'We shan't be more'n a couple of hours,' said Mr Braithwaite, reaching out through the window to proffer a pound note. The attendant's hand moved slowly to take it, but his jaw was slack as he stared at the apparition on the roof. He pressed the change-button, and a tenpenny piece popped out of the machine, followed by another and still another, then by a whole cascade like a fruit machine hitting the jackpot, crashing in a silver stream to the floor.

As the scarecrow jumped down and ran away the attendant suddenly realized what was happening, whipped his finger off the change-button, and stared sadly at the coins rolling round the car park .

'In you go,' he said, taking off his peaked cap, 'I'm quitting. When you start seeing things ... Well, I reckon it's time to pack the job in.'

'Right, you two,' said Mr Braithwaite as they left the car park, 'Do you want to tag along with Dolly and me, or go off exploring on your own?'

'Go off on our own, please,' said John eagerly.

Sue nodded.

'Be sure to meet us at one o'clock, then. Sharp, mind. Under the market clock. We'll all have a bite to eat,' he finished as the children scampered away hand in hand.

The farmer and his wife stared affectionately after them, held hands themselves, and set off more sedately for the town centre.

As the children reached the main street of the little town, bustling with shoppers, the scarecrow, yards ahead of them on the other side of the road, was peering into the windows of an employment agency, looking puzzled. He dug a sharp elbow into the ribs of a man standing near him.

'What be all they about in there then, mister?'

The man gave him an odd look. 'They're all about jobs, aren't they? Some from people who want jobs, and some from firms who want to give them work.'

'Oo-ah? There ain't one in there, I don't s'pose, from an 'ard-workin' respeckerble woman as wants a full-time job as a wife?'

The other man sneered. 'It's an employment agency! Not a marriage bureau! Can't you read?'

'Course I can read,' said the scarecrow, affronted, 'when I got my readin' 'ead on. Only this is my thinkin' 'ead as I brought along o' me today.'

As Worzel Gummidge shambled off down the street with his nose in the air, the other man stared at his back, wondering what to make of his last remark and decided, on the whole, that it was best to ignore it, and walked quickly away in the opposite direction.

On the other side of the street, as John stopped to

gaze wistfully into a toyshop window, Sue gasped and grabbed his arm. 'Crikey!' she hissed.

'What's up?'

'Look!' she answered, pointing dramatically across the road to where the scarecrow was standing outside the window of Upjohn and Stanley's Department Store, admiring the display.

'How did *he* get into town?'

'What's he come *for*? That's more important!' said John, taking his sister's hand and leading her carefully across the zebra crossing.

They found Worzel Gummidge enraptured, staring at a display of woollens, and in particular at an elaborate, colourful Fair Isle pullover slap bang in the centre of the window display.

'Hello, Worzel,' said Sue nervously.

'What are *you* doing in town?' John added.

'And isn't that Mr Braithwaite's best hat?'

'*And* Harry's gloves?'

'*And* Mrs Braithwaite's scarf?'

The scarecrow managed to tear his attention away from the window, but in his usual rude fashion he didn't bother with their questions.

'Bless me vest an' britches,' he croaked, 'but that's really summat is that there article, really summat!'

'What's that, Worzel?' Sue asked.

'Why, that there woolly, o'course. You ain't gone blind, 'ave 'ee? Don't the sight of a beautiful woolly like that set all the straw in your innards twitchin'?'

They looked with him into the window.

John nodded. 'It's a Fair Isle pullover.'

'A what d'ee say 'tis?'

'A Fair Isle pullover.'

'Dang me,' said the scarecrow, 'I *knowed* it was! A fair ol' pullover. Soon as I clapped eyes on it I says to meself, I says, that there's a fair ol' pullover if ever I saw 'un. I reckons if I 'ad a fair ol' pullover like that there, there wouldn't be a crow as'd come within 'undred mile o' me. A scarecrow as 'ad a fair ol' pullover like that would get a 'ard-workin' wife for 'isself, no bother, quick as winkin'. Allus providin' 'e 'ad 'is winkin' 'ead on, o' course. What's that there sign say above that pully?'

John read it out to him. 'This week's giveaway priced bargain.'

The scarecrow weighed it up. 'Do it now? I reckon as I'll 'ave one o' them there fair ol' pullovers then. For meself.'

Sue looked nervous, knowing quite well what was going through the scarecrow's mind. 'Have you got any money?' she asked.

'Money?' Worzel Gummidge barked. 'What do 'ee need money for? 'E just said, they're givin' them there fair ol' pullovers away in there.'

'Giveaway *prices*, Worzel,' said Sue anxiously. 'It doesn't mean they're giving things away *free*.'

'I know what it means, young missy. Don't matter if you say it in Yakkity nor Welsh nor Romany. Give away means give away, so it does. An' if you's tellin' me as they're givin' away them fair ol' pullovers but keepin' 'em back from scarecrows, well then! I'll go in there an' kick up a rare ol' fuss, just you see if I don't!'

'But Worzel!' cried John – but it was too late. With a fixed expression the scarecrow was already striding purposefully forward through the door of the shop.

Sue shook her head.

'Crikey!' she whispered.

'Crikey *Moses*!' echoed her brother.

As he left his tricycle in the unattended car park, the Crowman noticed the green glass bottle on the seat of the Braithwaites' car, and slipped it into his pocket with a slow smile.

On the other side of the street, as the farmer slipped into the tobacconist's for an ounce of shag, Mrs Braithwaite stood smiling on the pavement, watching the world go by.

Suddenly, in the window of Upjohn and Stanley's Department Store, a curious figure with straw dangling from one sleeve caught her eye, and she tugged at her husband's sleeve as he emerged. 'Jack,' she hissed urgently, 'look over there!'

Mr Braithwaite peered across the road in the direction of her outstretched finger.

'Where? What am I supposed to be looking at? I can't see anything.'

Mrs Braithwaite shook her head. 'Neither can I. Not now. But just a moment ago, when you were in that shop...'

'Well,' he prompted, 'What was it?'

'I know you'll only laugh at me, Jack, but I've got to

tell you this. When you were in there, I could've sworn I saw the scarecrow from Ten-acre Field, going in that shop.'

The farmer laughed a rich, deep-throated laugh. 'Did you indeed? And what would my scarecrow be doing in Littleminster High Street in the middle of the morning? Anyway, looking at that place reminds me – I could do with a new pair of gloves.' He took her arm to guide her across the road.

Inside the shop, Worzel Gummidge was deep in a one-sided conversation with a dummy in a wedding dress.

'Oo-ah! You're a bit of a beauty an' no mistake,' he nodded approvingly. 'Yes, young woman, you can stick your nose in the air if you like, but you wait till I got me fair ol' pullie on! You won't be so toffee-nosed then, I bet. I reckon I might even axe 'ee to marry me, so I might!' he concluded, heading for the Menswear Department, where the floor manager was rubbing his aching neck.

His young assistant looked at him solicitously.

'Your sore neck giving you trouble again, Mr Mooney?' she asked.

'Never mind my neck, Miss Simmons,' he snapped, rather abruptly, 'There's a dirty, disgusting tramp drooling over your Fair Isle sweaters!'

The girl looked vaguely in Worzel Gummidge's direction. 'Ooooh!' she squeaked. 'Do you think I've made a sale?'

The floor manager snorted.

'Of course not! The rascal's obviously penniless.

Drunk too, I shouldn't wonder! Ignore the filthy fellow and with a little bit of luck he'll go away. *Ow!*' he winced as his neck gave another twinge.

'Very good, Mr Mooney.'

'And while you're ignoring him, Miss Simmons, you can put your gentlemen's cardigans in order. Just look as them! The 38 to 40s are all mixed up with the 42 to 44s!'

The girl bit her lip nervously. 'I'm very sorry, Mr Mooney,' she said, looking anxious as the scarecrow fingered her pullovers.

'Ignore him, Miss Simmons,' insisted Mr Mooney; 'whatever he does, pay no attention to him at all,' and he marched away to inspect some thermal underpants.

The scarecrow looked around for service and spotted Miss Simmons.

'Oy! missus!' he bellowed. 'Can 'ee 'ear me? I wants one o' these 'ere fair ol' pullovers as you's givin' away. Can 'ee parcel one up in some fair ol' string an' wrappin' paper so's I can carry it away?'

When the girl turned her back on him and studied the far wall he sniffed angrily.

'Dang silly woman's deaf as a dead crow. Well, if she ain't goin' to serve me, stands to reason as I'll 'ave to serve meself. An' if I can't 'ave a fair ol' pullover all wrapped up I'll just 'ave to wear 'un now,' he decided, picking one up and starting to struggle into it.

Hunting round the store for him, John and Sue came into the Menswear Department just as Worzel Gummidge's stalky fingers began to get impossibly tangled up in the wool.

'Oooo-ah! Oooo-ah!' he grunted, 'Come on then, dang pesky thing! Get on with 'ee. Ain't no wonder they're 'avin' to give these fair ol' pullovers away. Dang pesky tarnation things don't go on a body no 'ow! Danger to man an' scarecrow so they are! Didn't ought to be allowed! Dunno 'bout fair ol' pullovers – more like rotten ol' pullovers if you axe me! Oo-ah!'

'He *must* be around here somewhere,' whispered John, peering round a tie rack.

'There are the pullovers, John, and ... Oh!' gasped Sue as they caught sight of the scarecrow, by now inextricably entwined, thrashing about inside the pullover in his weird scarecrow fashion. 'What are we going to *do*?' she demanded.

John shrugged. 'What *can* we do?'

'We've got to go and help him, John, He'll get into a terrible tangle if we don't.'

'If you ask me he's in a terrible tangle now,' said John, as Worzel Gummidge froze at the floor manager's approach.

'Much better, Miss Simmons!' he beamed. 'A hundred and one per cent improvement in those cardigans.'

'Thank you, Mr Mooney,' she replied. 'Er ... Mr Mooney? That old tramp. He won't go away!'

'Ignore him, Miss Simmons,' said the floor manager blandly, his back to the scarecrow, 'as I am doing. Pretend he isn't there. Look in the opposite direction.'

'But he's ... he's behaving rather oddly, Mr. Mooney.'

The floor manager looked smug. 'All the more

reason, Miss Simmons, to pretend that he isn't there. Oddly in what way?' he frowned.

'He's got one of my Fair Isle pullovers over his head. And he isn't *moving*, Mr Mooney,' she said nervously.

Fearful of what he would see, Mr Mooney turned slowly round and took in the sight of the scarecrow, with a brightly-coloured pullover pulled over his head, and his arms rigidly outstretched in the correct scarecrow pose, leaning back against the counter.

'Really!' he exploded. 'That is going a bit too far, Miss Simmons. I mean, I'm all for turning a blind eye, but there is a bally limit!' and he strode forward, the girl at his heels.

'Return that pullover to the counter at once!' he ordered. 'Do you hear me, my man? Hand over that garment before I summon the store detective and have you charged with theft!'

There was no response from the deeply-sulking scarecrow.

'You don't suppose there's anything wrong with him, do you, Mr Mooney?' Miss Simmons asked. 'He's very quiet.'

The floor manager turned up his nose. 'Drunk, most probably, I shouldn't wonder. They're like that, tramps. There'll be something wrong with him before *I've* finished with him! I'll teach the rascal to play hide and seek inside one of our woollen garments!'

'Oooh!' cooed Miss Simmons, impressed by the floor manager's determined manner. 'What are you going to do, Mr Mooney?'

'*We*, Miss Simmons,' he replied, 'are going to take repossession of that pullover!'

'Coo-er! Are we really?'

'We most certainly are. Forward, Miss Simmons, and remove that pullover from his head!' he ordered.

The girl was suddenly a lot less impressed. '*Me*, Mister Mooney?' she asked.

'Who else? While *I* keep an eye on him. And both hands free,' he added reassuringly, 'in case he should attempt physical violence. Get on with it, girl! I'm standing by and in full control. You have nothing to fear, have you?'

'*No*, Mr Mooney,' said Miss Simmons, who had decided her floor manager was a rotten coward after all.

She approached the scarecrow and began to fiddle tentatively with the sleeves of the pullover, trying to tug them over his outstretched fingers.

'Oooh!' she squealed, 'He ain't got no fingers, Mr Mooney! He's got twigs!' Her initial revulsion disappeared and she peered underneath the pullover.

'Would you believe it!' she giggled. 'He's not a tramp at all, Mr Mooney!

The floor manager looked severe. 'Do *not* contradict me, Miss Simmons. I have been in the retail trade long enough, I hope, to be able to tell a tramp from an ordinary customer.'

'He's not a customer either, Mr Mooney! Not unless we've started serving scarecrows!' and she hauled the pullover free from the turnippy head.

The floor manager's eyes popped. 'Great Heavens! A scarecrow in the Menswear Department of Upjohn and Stanley's? How on earth did it get here? And what would Mr Upjohn say,' he added nervously, 'if he were to walk through the store now and see it? Let alone Mr Stanley?'

'*What*,' boomed a voice from behind string vests, 'Would Mr Upjohn say if he were to see *what*, Mr Mooney?' and Mr Stanley emerged to confront the perspiring floor manager.

'Oh! Er ... Good afternoon, Mr Stanley,' he stammered, trying to stand in front of the scarecrow. 'I was just remarking to Miss Simmons, sir, as to ... er ... as to whether you'd had a chance yet to observe our remarkable display of woollen menswear garments?'

'I have that on my schedule for this afternoon, Mr Mooney. Now what's that behind your back?' frowned Mr Stanley.

Mr Mooney giggled nervously. 'There's nothing behind my back, Mr Stanley. Nothing at all! I wonder if you'd care to step outside now, sir, and enjoy our fabulous window display of woollen menswear garments?'

Mr Stanley looked stern. 'Not *yet*, Mr Mooney. Now. There *is* something behind your back. If you please ...'

'Sir, it could *rain* this afternoon,' gabbled Mr Mooney desperately. 'It *will* rain, Mr Stanley, I heard them say so on the weather forecast – heavy thunder in the western region!'

'There will be severe storms in the Menswear Department,' growled Mr Stanley, 'if you don't step aside and show me what you're concealing.'

Hanging his head, the floor manager shuffled sideways. Miss Simmons said brightly, 'It's a scarecrow, Mr Stanley!'

'A scarecrow?'

Mr Mooney nodded, fearing the worst. 'I'm afraid so, Mr Stanley,' he whimpered.

'What a wonderful idea!' beamed Mr Stanley.

Mr Mooney burbled on, still apologizing as though Mr Stanley hadn't spoken. 'I am most *abjectly* sorry, Mr Stanley, and I do apologize *most* humbly, but I had not the slightest idea that a ... *what* did you say?' he gasped.

'Brilliant, Mr Mooney! I never knew you had it in you. To go out and acquire a real scarecrow for the outdoors display in the Gardening Department!'

Mr Mooney gaped. 'Did I, sir! I mean yes I did, yes, Mr Stanley, sir!' he babbled as Miss Simmons gave him a black look.

'It's a *wonderful* scarecrow, Mr Mooney, truly wonderful! Just look! Look here – a real bird's nest in the pocket!'

Mr Mooney pulled himself together and decided to make the most of his stroke of good fortune. 'Has it, Mr Stanley? I mean, yes, it has! I chose one with a bird's nest, *specifically*.'

'Was it difficult to find, Mr Stanley?'

Mr Mooney looked modest. 'Mmmmm, not easy sir, but for Upjohn and Stanley's,' he added smarmily, 'nothing is too much trouble!'

Mr Stanley frowned professionally. 'I don't think that the hat's quite right, Mr Mooney, and the scarf doesn't really suit either. But those gloves! Those gloves are a joy to behold! And the face! The face is perfect, quite perfect.'

For a moment there was just a gleam of life in the scarecrow's eyes.

'It's a truly remarkable scarecrow's face, Mooney. Exquisite. Do you know, I think it really is quite the ugliest thing I have ever seen in all my life?' decided Mr Stanley, as Worzel Gummidge, satisfied with the verdict, froze once more into turnippy immobility. 'Take it over to the Gardening Department at once, Mr Mooney. That scarecrow will be the centrepiece of the entire Upjohn and Stanley outdoor display!'

As the two children followed at a safe distance, the scarecrow was lugged clumsily across the store to the Gardening Department, where it was propped up in the middle of yards of artificial grass, festooned with watering cans, spades, forks and secateurs. When the staff had finished they crept forward and stood in front of the display staring up at him.

'How *are* we going to rescue him from this lot?' asked John despairingly.

'We can't. He's very quiet,' said Sue. 'Do you think he's still sulking?'

The scarecrow growled. 'If you pesky tichy yewmans can't tell the differ 'tween a scarecrow as is sulkin' an' a scarecrow as is proud to be doin' a fair ol' job in the retail trade you dunno much about scarecrows, so you don't, thass all I got to say! Iggerant kids! Dunno what they'm supposed to teach 'em in school these days!'

'If you're going to be rude, Worzel,' said Sue angrily, 'don't expect us to help you!'

'If'n I need any titchy yewman's 'elp, young missy, I'll axe fer it! Not as it's likely to be yourn. But I ain't 'ere to talk to customers. I'm too important for that, so I am. I'm a Centrepiece, so *I* am! Oo-ah! I 'eard 'im say that!'

The scarecrow's nose went up in the air, and he became rigid and lifeless. Saddened and insulted, the two children crept away to look for the toy department, leaving the scarecrow alone.

But only for a moment: just as he was getting to like his work, Mr and Mrs Braithwaite appeared, and stopped in their tracks as they spotted him.

'Well! If you couldn't knock me down with a feather! *Now* tell me I need a new pair of glasses!' gasped Mrs Braithwaite.

'You *do* need a new pair of glasses,' replied her husband gently.

'Happen I do, for reading. I'm not denying it. But my eyesight's good enough to know a scarecrow when I see one. And is that or isn't that our scarecrow from Ten-acre Field?'

They moved forward and peered closely at Worzel Gummidge's face. Mr Braithwaite didn't really want to believe what he saw. 'No, no,' he said, 'p'raps it does bear a *passing* resemblance to our'n, I'll admit that, Dolly, but it can't *be* our'n, now can it?'

'*Why* can't it?' demanded Mrs Braithwaite stubbornly.

'Because *you* know, and *I* know, that *our* Ten-acre

Field scarecrow is scaring off crows in Ten-acre Field,'
he replied slowly, as much to reassure himself as his
wife.

She shook her head, far from convinced. 'I tell you
that's *it*, Jack.'

'No, ours hasn't got gloves. And it hasn't got a hat
like that.'

He peered closer. 'Just a minute! Well I'm blessed!
That's *my* hat! That's my best tweedy hat that I lost
this morning!'

Dolly gasped. 'And that's my scarf too! And that *is*
our scarecrow, Jack! I tell you, we ought to see somebody and complain.'

The oily voice of Mr Stanley crept up on them un-
awares. 'Complain, madam?' he said greasily. 'Complain is a word we don't expect to hear at Upjohn and
Stanley's!'

Mrs Braithwaite puffed herself up and looked him
squarely in the eye.

'You've heard it now!' she said angrily, 'And if we
don't get satisfaction from you I'll go right to the top.
I'll see Mr Upjohn himself and tell him too.'

Mr Stanley inclined his head to her in a little bow.
'I may not be the illustrious Mr Upjohn, madam, but
I do have the honour to be the other partner. My name
is Stanley. Now, what seems to be the trouble?'

Mrs Braithwaite wasn't at all impressed by his
placatory manner.

'I want that scarecrow! That is to say,' she added,
'*we* want that scarecrow.'

Mr Stanley waved his hands in a gesture of regret.

'Ah! Now there I have to disappoint you, madam. The scarecrow is only for display.'

The farmer's wife advanced and prodded him in the chest with her umbrella. 'We don't want to buy it! We mean to *take* it. It's our scarecrow. It was stolen from our field!'

Her husband whipped his hat off the scarecrow's head and handed it to Mr Stanley.

'You take a look inside that hat,' he said with an air of triumph, 'If you don't believe us. Go on. You tell me what it's got written in there?'

Turning the hat over, Mr Stanley read out the name tag. 'J ... M ... Braithwaite.'

The farmer tapped his own chest. 'Right,' he announced. 'That's me. Jock Muscroft Braithwaite.'

'And if you'll take the trouble to examine that scarf,' went on his wife, pressing home the attack, you'll see that's got a name tag on it, too. Dolly Braithwaite. That's me. I'm his wife.'

The farmer looked stern. 'And if you're requiring any *more* proof as to who he belongs to. I can bring along my farm labourer and a whole village full of folk who'll be more than willing to tell you he belongs to me.'

A worried expression crept over Mr Stanley's face as he realized that some sort of mistake had been made.

'Oh, come now, Mr Braithwaite,' he said, forcing a smile, 'I don't think we need to go to those lengths. Clearly some error has occurred. I expect one of our van-men picked up the wrong scarecrow. If you'll just step along to the office I'm sure all this can be sorted out quite amicably. After all, we're not going to fall out over a common-or-garden dirty old scarecrow, are we?' he finished, leading Mr and Mrs Braithwaite off to the offices on the top floor.

Worzel Gummidge's face clouded over. 'Dirty?' he croaked. 'Old? I ain't stoppin' 'ere perched up on no plastic grass to be insulted, so I ain't. I ain't no common-or-garden scarecrow neither! I'm a field scarecrow! Allus was an' allus will be. An' the sooner I gets back to Ten-acre Field, it seems to me, the better off I'll be!' and with trowels and buckets dangling and clattering all over him he stepped down from his stand and stamped angrily off the display.

As Worzel Gummidge was leaving the display in the Gardening Department, the Crowman, as if following in his tracks, was just coming into Menswear, where Mr Mooney's stiff neck was making him really irritable, and he was again upbraiding the unfortunate Miss Simmons.

'*Do* make some attempt to tidy up your glove counter, Miss Simmons,' he moaned. 'it's all at sixes and sevens, especially the seven-and-a-half and eights.' He broke off suddenly as he caught sight of the browsing Crowman. 'Bless my soul,' he whispered anxiously. 'There's another tramp! Perhaps it's a disguise! They may be an international gang of menswear thieves!'

But Miss Simmons wasn't paying any attention; a jerky movement had caught her eye in another part of the shop; she had turned to see what it was, and now stared open-mouthed at Worzel Gummidge, creeping through Soft Furnishings towards the exit.

'There's the first one, Mr Mooney!' she cried. 'The one got up as a scarecrow! He's making off with the gardenware!'

Mr Mooney turned quickly to look, winced with pain as his neck locked, and grabbed the girl's arm. 'Oh! Ah!' he yelped. 'Get me a chair, Miss Simmons!'

As the floor manager lowered himself gingerly into a chair the Crowman came forward, doffing his hat politely.

'Perhaps I may be of some assistance, sir?' he suggested.

The floor manager looked up at him sourly, and the effort of doing so made his neck hurt even more. 'I don't want you!' he snapped. 'Miss Simmons, summon the store's first aid assistant, then summon the store detective while I –'

He broke off and fell silent as the Crowman held his eyes with a mesmeric gaze.

'Easy does it, Mr Mooney . . .'

The floor manager gasped. 'How do you know my name?'

'There's nothing wrong with you that a couple of drops of this won't cure,' went on the Crowman, taking the little green glass bottle from his pocket.

He shook two drops onto his fingertips and lightly touched the other man's neck. The effect was instantaneous: his neck immediately unlocked and as he waggled his head experimentally once or twice, a beam of delight spread over his incredulous face.

'It works!' he exclaimed. 'It really works!'

'It *always* works,' said the Crowman gently.

Mr Stanley had appeared on the scene and watched all that had happened.

'Might one inquire, my good man,' he purred, 'whether the recipe for that formula is for sale?'

The black-clothed figure shook his head with a sad smile. 'I'm sorry, Mr Stanley ...'

'How d'you know my name?' he frowned.

The Crowman ignored the question. '... but I'm sworn to secrecy,' he continued. 'It's an old country herbal liniment, and was handed down to me by a Westmorland washerwoman who'd had it handed down to her by a wandering Welsh gypsy of royal Romany blood.'

As the Crowman lifted his hat in salutation and made his way out of the store in pursuit of the scarecrow, Miss Simmons, Mr Stanley and Mr Mooney stood silent, staring at his back, quite bewildered by the strange figure.

Outside the shop, the Crowman's big black tricycle was waiting at the kerb, a dusty town sparrow sitting on the handlebars. He cocked his head to one side to listen to the chattering bird, then nodded, climbed aboard, and pedalled slowly away towards the village.

Inside the car, as they sped through the countryside, John and Sue were agog to hear all that had happened between the Braithwaites and Mr Stanley.

'Well,' said the farmer's wife, 'he didn't say a whole

lot, really. Only that he was puzzled as to how the scarecrow got there. And that he'd send it back as soon as possible. In one of their vans.'

'He can't send it back too soon for me,' muttered her husband, 'I need that scarecrow in Ten-acre Field.'

He slowed down and peered through the windscreen at a black-clad figure on the road ahead. 'Isn't that that Crowman fellow?' he asked.

The children nodded eagerly and turned to wave as they overtook him. He waved back, a slow smile on his face as he stared up at the car's roof-rack and saw Worzel Gummidge raise his hat to him.

'Oh, Worzel, Worzel, what am I to do with you?' he laughed, as the little car pottered out of sight round the bend and silence descended on the road once more.

CHAPTER 4
A Little Learning

THE summer passed, as summers must, and gave way to the first damp, drizzly days of autumn. The green leaves faded on the trees and become yellow and brown, drifting lazily down through the mist to form thick wet carpets in the lanes. The swallows gathered on the telephone wires, lined up in families and flocks, ready to set off for the Mediterranean sun, and as the days grew short and the yellow sun began to set earlier and earlier the children found that school time had come round.

'It's not a *bad* school,' said John after the first couple of weeks, as they kicked up the fallen leaves in the lane on their way home. They had new uniforms, blue blazers and satchels, and wore shiny black wellington boots.

Sue nodded. 'Mmm. It's not *that* boring,' she agreed. 'I suppose it could be worse.'

At the farmyard gate Harry looked up from his work. ''Ave a good day at school?' he asked, putting down his bucket of pig-swill and easing his aching back.

'Not bad,' John admitted.

'Ah. Well. Your Dad's 'ad to go into the village to do a job. And Mr Braithwaite's had to run Mrs Braithwaite somewhere in the car. Only before she went out she asked me to be sure and tell you to keep out of mischief till she gets back. Message received and understood?' he asked with a smile.

'Message received and understood, Harry,' grinned Sue.

The farm labourer looked around the yard. 'And if you want something to keep you out of mischief, you can help me,' he suggested.

The children looked suspicious. Most of Harry's jobs were messy and smelly and involved getting close to pigs. 'What doing, Harry?' asked John.

He scratched his head as he answered. 'By having a good scout round for a big ball of string I brought out here with me. I promised to tie up those poles over there for Mr Braithwaite, only my string's gone missing.'

A thought crossed his mind. 'Hey! It weren't you two as nicked it was it?'

Sue looked indignant. 'Course not!'

'We've only just got back from school,' John added. 'You saw us come in.'

There was a twinkle in the labourer's eyes as he saw that the children really were telling the truth. 'Well, I believe you,' he confessed, 'though thousands wouldn't. But, if you do set eyes on it, it belongs to me.'

As Harry turned back to his work the children climbed the short flight of wooden steps to the caravan door and let themselves in, carefully hauling off their wet wellingtons and parking them in the boot box inside the door.

'Well *I'm* not spending the afternoon looking for Harry's ball of string,' said Sue, slipping off her new blazer and tossing it and her satchel aside. 'I fancy going to look for Worzel.'

'He wasn't in Ten-acre Field. Not when we came past,' John pointed out. He climbed out of his own blazer and hung both it and his sister's tidily away in the wardrobe. 'He's probably in the barn; you know how he creeps in there whenever it gets wet.'

Sue wriggled her grey woollen dress off over her head. 'Well, if we're going in the barn *I'm* putting my jeans on,' she announced. 'You know how Dad goes on if we get anything messed up.'

With a sigh, John agreed, pulling off his shirt and shorts and looking for his own jeans. '*And* if we leave a mess in here,' he added pointedly. 'So, hang your dress up.'

Inside the barn, as the children slipped in, carefully closing the heavy wooden door behind them, it was gloomy and still. There was a rustling of straw from the loft, and after a moment the sound of a tetchy croaking voice.

'Pesky danged thing's in 'ere somewhere, I knows it is.'

Sue nudged her brother, 'He's up there!'

The scarecrow's voice continued. 'Danged if I don't reckon as I'll manage without it if the pesky thing don't turn up soon. Rotten ol' nuisance it is an' no mistake. Better off without it, so I am.'

The children crept to the ladder and looked up at

the pile of hay in the loft, heaving and tossing as the scarecrow burrowed through it.

'Worzel,' called Sue softly, 'are you there?'

The pile of hay froze into stillness.

'You can sulk as much as you want,' added John, 'but we know you're up there.'

The hay shifted. The scarecrow's head popped out and glared down at them. 'I ain't talkin' to you three pesky kids, so you'm got no call to come pesterin' round me,' he barked.

'We haven't done anything,' said Sue indignantly.

'Ar. That's 'alf your trouble. Not doin' nothin'. I been lookin' for you three all arternoon.'

'We aren't *three*,' said John wearily. 'We're *two*. And we had to go to school. Term's started.'

Worzel Gummidge scowled.

'Never tol' me nothin' 'bout no school, so 'ee didn't. Orter 'ave known I would'a needed 'ee. Thought that was obvious.'

Sue adopted an air of reasonableness. 'We don't know anything's wrong unless you *tell* us, Worzel. What's the matter?' she finished, leading the way up the ladder to the loft.

'I lorst me right arm, that's what's the matter,' grumbled the scarecrow. 'I comes in 'ere to put a new bit o' straw in me left leg, on account o' I'm gettin' a bit o' damp an' field-mice in the ol' stuffin', it bein' that time o' year, and afore I knows it, dang pesky arm drops off an' 'ides isself, so it do.'

The children dived into the straw and burrowed along the length of the loft together. It was warm and musty and quite dark under the dry straw, and they kept bumping into one another.

'I've got it!' cried John in a muffled yell.

'That's not Worzel's arm,' Sue complained, 'it's my leg! And anyway, *I've* found it,' she said triumphantly, scrabbling out and holding the lost arm aloft. 'Here it is!'

She examined it and handed it back to the scarecrow.

'Your hand's got Harry's string in it,' she said accusingly.

'Course it 'as,' agreed the scarecrow, screwing the arm back into place. 'Can't stuff a leg without some string to tie it off with, can 'ee?'

'Harry's looking everywhere for that string,' said Sue. 'He's very cross.'

'Wait till 'e's lorst 'is arm,' sneered Worzel Gummidge, 'then 'e'll really 'ave summat to complain about. Specially if there ain't no one there to 'elp 'im look for it. All at *school*.'

Sue sat down on a bale of hay, drew her knees up to her chin, and wrapped her arms around them. 'Well, didn't you ever have to go to school then, Worzel?' she asked.

'Never 'ad no need to, young missy,' he replied, examining his arm critically. 'That was 'cos I 'ad this very clever 'ead once what taught me all manner o' things.'

'Where did you get it from?'

'It wor a Christmas prezzie what I got given by the Crowman. Now that 'ead were always 'anging around schools, so it were, pickin' up all kinds o' facts. Weren't no more nor an ol' turnip, but that tarnation pesky 'ead were clever! Learned me 'istory, so it did, an' geography, an' it learned me no end o' things about shepherdin' sheep.'

John looked sceptical. 'Could it do mathematics?'

'Oo-ah! I 'spect it could. If I knowed what mathymatics was.'

'You know,' said Sue. 'Arithmetic. Sums. Adding things up and taking them away.'

'Oo-ah! It would do that there all right.'

He wrinkled his pointed nose with the effort of remembering what his clever head had taught him. 'Two sheep an' three sheep is five sheep!' he said brightly.

'Fantastic,' jeered John.

Worzel Gummidge warmed to it. 'An' four taties an' five taties is eight taties! 'Ow's that?'

The children exchanged a glance, concealing their grins. 'Hmm, near enough,' said Sue charitably. 'Could it do tables?'

The scarecrow shook his head sadly.

'To be strictly honest it were never that good on tables. Nor on chairs neither. Matter o' fact it weren't much good at addin' up any kind of furniture. Three tables an' five tables I've tried addin' up, but I keep comin' up wi' the answer's a wardrobe. I give up on furniture with it in the end, so I did. But on sheep an' taties it wor red 'ot.'

'What happened to it?' asked Sue.

The scarecrow's face fell, then darkened in annoyance as he spoke.

'I lorst *that* an' all. No, I tell a lie. I 'id it. I 'id that 'ead somewhere safe. I didn't want to lose it, see? On account o' it bein' so pesky clever. Matter o' fact it wor that 'ead isself as thought o' its own 'idin' place. Trouble is I ain't never 'ad another 'ead since as was clever enough to find it.'

'P'raps you'd be just as clever, Worzel, if you went to school like us,' suggested Sue.

The scarecrow scowled.

''Ow many times do I 'ave to tell 'ee, young missy? I dang well don't need to go to no school. Not with an 'ead as clever as what I got 'idden away.'

'But what's the good of having a clever head if you don't know where it is?' she pointed out.

There was a loud banging from outside as Mrs Braithwaite, back from her shopping, hammered on a frying pan with a wooden spoon.

'Tea's ready, children! Come along!' she called.

'We'll have to go, Worzel,' sighed Sue, 'but we'll come and look for you tomorrow.'

The scarecrow looked grumpy.

'Mebbe you'll find me an' mebbe you won't,' he muttered as the children clattered down the ladder out of the loft. 'Depends on whether I chooses to see 'ee three.'

'There's only *two* of us! I told you before!' called John as they dragged the heavy barn door shut behind them.

The scarecrow considered going into a sulk, but decided that it wasn't worth the bother, not with nobody around to see.

'Proper little smartipants, that there titchy pesky yewman thinks 'e is. But if I can find that there clever 'ead, 'appen I'll teach 'im a thing or three! Dang me if I don't!'

The next day, as the sun tried to melt the morning mist, the children hopped down the damp steps of the caravan swinging their satchels. Wearing the apron he wore when he did the drying up their father came to the caravan door to see them off.

'And you two watch your step today,' he called good-naturedly, ' 'cos I'll be keeping an eye on you!'

'*You?* How d'you mean, Dad?' asked John.

Their father grinned.

'Mr Braithwaite's got me another little job; I'll be fixing some slates on the school roof this afternoon. And I'll be looking out for you. Cheerio, then,' he waved, as they slipped through the gate and out of sight.

He made his way back into the pretty little caravan and got on with his chores, humming to himself.

There was a sudden thumping, banging noise that seemed to come from under the caravan, and made his tidily-stacked plates rattle.

'Gordon Bennet!' he muttered, grabbing at a tottering tea-cup, 'I'll bet that's Harry's dog again, burying something under the caravan.' He stamped hard on the caravan's wooden floor. 'Go on! Get off out of it, you mangy brute!'

Beneath the caravan, crawling among the old buckets and empty petrol cans, Worzel Gummidge shook his head as dust and dirt dislodged by Mr Peter's stamping drifted down and settled in his straw.

'Dang pesky bangin',' he muttered angrily, ''Ow'm I expected to find a missin' 'ead, with all that there stampin' goin' on? Now ... Did I 'ide it under 'ere or did I 'ide it somewheres else?'

He tipped over a couple of rusty old buckets and clattered them together to see if the clever head would fall out, but there was nothing there.

'Dang pesky 'ead. If it's that clever, 'ow come it didn't tell me where it's 'idden 'isself?'

Above his head, Mr Peters was also losing his temper, annoyed by the banging and clattering below.

'Oh, *damn* that dog!' he shouted, grabbing a broom and banging the floor. 'Shut up!'

Crawling on his belly the scarecrow wriggled out from under the caravan and emerged into the thin sunlight. He rubbed his ears.

'Dang fool near deafened me, so 'e did. Got no right to go bangin' around on floors when respeckerble scarecrows is crawlin' underneath 'em,' he muttered.

He grabbed a clod of earth, hurled it in through the open window of the caravan, and stumped grumpily off across the farmyard.

Inside the caravan, Mr Peters bellowed as the clod of earth caught him on the side of the head.

'What the dickens!' he shouted, rushing out.

There was no one to be seen.

He looked round the farmyard, ran down the steps, and caught sight of Harry in the distance by the pigsties.

'Harry!' be bellowed. 'Where's that dog of yours?'

The farm labourer looked puzzled.

''Appen she's back at the cottage, Mr Peters. Leastways, she was when I left 'er!'

'Are you sure she hasn't just thrown a damn great clod of earth through my caravan window?'

Harry looked sadly at Mr Peters, and decided that he was obviously losing his grip.

'No, Mr Peters,' he said earnestly. 'She don't throw things. Not a lot.'

As Mr Peters stamped angrily back into the caravan to clean up the mess, Mr Braithwaite emerged round the corner of the barns carrying two heavy buckets of pig-swill in his brawny hands. Parking them on the cobbles of the yard by the pigsties he called to Harry.

'I put the swill down outside the sty, Harry. You can give it to 'em whenever you like,' and made his way back across the yard and into the kitchen.

Careless of discovery, the scarecrow strolled into the farmyard again and gazed down on the fat, pink, grunting, honking pigs.

'I wonder if that danged 'ead told me to 'ide it inside the pigsty?' he mused, then shook his head decisively. 'No, wouldn't do that, so it wouldn't. It were too danged clever by 'alf. It was a turnip 'ead an' it would'a knowed danged well as them there tarnation pigs would'a et it up.' He glanced down and saw the buckets of pig-swill.

'Mind you,' he speculated, 'it could'a 'idden 'isself in a bucket. Turnip 'ead'd fit snug an' neat in a bucket, so it would.' Picking up a bucket he sniffed at it, swilled it round, and dumped the sloppy contents on the cobbles.

'Oo-ah!' he grumbled. ''Tain't in that 'un, so it ain't.' He repeated the process with the second bucket, splashing his black boots with pig-swill.

''Tain't in that 'un, neither,' he said sadly, tossing the shiny new bucket aside and wandering away.

The farm labourer clambered over the stone wall of the pigsty and caught sight of the upended buckets.

'Now who'd do a daft thing like that?' he muttered, staring at the slowly-spreading pool of pig-swill.

Across the farmyard, nearer to the caravan, Mrs Braithwaite emerged from the kitchen door with a round wicker basket full of washing and set it down on the cobbles under the washing line. Her plump hand plunged into her apron pocket.

'Oh!' she scolded herself. 'Where's my clothes pegs?' And she hurried away, back to the farmhouse.

The scarecrow's head appeared above the wall, and he vaulted over in an ungainly tangle of arms and legs.

'Oo-ah! I knows just what 'ee means, missus! Now that there basket looks a likely place for a turnip 'ead to 'ide isself in, so it does,' and he hoisted the big wicker basket over his head and dumped the contents all over the ground. He kicked at a pair of the farmer's underpants, and a whalebone corset.

'Dang pesky tarnation 'ead!' he complained. 'Don't deserve to 'ave isself found!'

As the scarecrow lurched disconsolately away across the farmyard and into the field, Mrs Braithwaite emerged from the kitchen. Her jaw dropped as she took in the sight of all her crisp, clean washing lying in the mud and muck of the farmyard.

'Jack!' she shouted. 'Jack! Just come and look here!'

Her husband galloped out of the house at the urgency of her words.

'Must be those kids,' he guessed wildly as he stared at the scattered washing.

'They're at *school*, Jack!' said his wife. 'It's impossible!'

On the far side of the wall, the scarecrow listened to their conversation and slowly raised his eyebrows.

'Oo-ah! Thass it! That dang school! *Thass* where I 'id it! Tarnation take it, I'm *sure* on it! Danged pesky 'ead were that fond o' learnin' things it wouldn't'a idden isself anywheres 'cept at that there school!'

In the village school, after break, the children bent their heads low over their maths books and applied themselves to their algebra problems, while Miss Jamieson, the schoolmistress, marked essays at her desk.

Outside, the scarecrow spotted the ladder that Mr Peters had been using and shinned up it towards the roof, pausing at the window of the schoolroom to glance in and see what was going on. A little girl, bored with algebra, looked up as he did so and gasped in surprise, attracting everyone else's attention.

'No talking, please,' said Miss Jamieson firmly as they giggled at the unfamiliar sight of the scarecrow's turnip face peering in. 'Get on with the work I set you!'

There was silence for a few moments, then one by one the children began to peer round their books at the window where the scarecrow, enjoying the effect his appearance caused, was pulling faces. The giggling came again, louder this time, and Miss Jamieson looked up, more angrily now.

'No *talking*,' she insisted. 'I mean it! Now, get on with your work!'

The scarecrow's face disappeared.

The children waited.

Very slowly, inch by inch, Worzel Gummidge lowered himself into view from above the window – upside down!

'Now stop it!' Miss Jamieson repeated as a wave of laughter rolled across the room. 'Otherwise I'll keep you all here in detention after school!'

As the laughter subsided to suppressed giggles she followed their eyes and caught sight of the scarecrow's hat waving good-bye.

'Right!' she cried. 'So that's it! Leave this to me, children, and remain *quite silent* while I'm away!' and she marched out of the room.

Scrambling about on the roof, the scarecrow muttered angrily to himself as he peered into gutters and felt inside disused house-martins' nests.

'Dang me, I *knows* it was somewheres 'ereabouts. I's looked for 'un everywheres from the cellar to the roof. There's only that there chimbley pot left –'

His eyes lit up.

'Oo-ah! O' course! The chimbley pot! *Thass* where I 'id it!' he cried, and crawling up the tiles of the roof he reached up to feel in a crevice between the two tall stacks.

'Oo-ah! I *knowed* it was up 'ere somewheres,' he breathed as his twiggy hand emerged with a sacking-wrapped bundle. 'I wonder if it's as clever as it allus was? Or whether the rain might o' got into it a bit up 'ere, made it go sort o' soggy?'

Straddling the roof, his legs dangling down on either side, he carefully unwrapped his parcel and examined with loving care the learned-looking head with the old cracked hornrimmed glasses hooked on its nose and the mortar-board perched on top.

'Looks all right, so it do,' he decided, brushing away a cobweb. 'Now I'll show them pesky kids what bein' clever really means!' and he looked around to see how he was going to get down again. The precipitous roof seemed steeper from above than it had from below and the ladder had disappeared.

He swung one leg over and gingerly lowered himself towards the guttering, then had second thoughts and hauled himself back with a puzzled frown.

'Dang sight harder gettin' down nor it were gettin' up, an' thass a fact,' he grumbled. 'Reckon I'll 'ave to use me clever 'ead now, 'stead o' savin' it till I gets back to Ten-acre Field,' and with great care he laid the head in his lap.

His workaday head came off quite easily; he put it down on the ledge of the chimney stack and eased and squeezed his clever head into place. He looked around in satisfaction and tried a couple of preliminary blinks.

'Now then, let's try 'un! Two times two is four. Ar. Three times two are six. Ar. Eight eights? Sixty-four, so they are!'

Settling back contentedly against the warm chimney-stack he folded his arms across his chest and wallowed in his new-found cleverness.

'Fourteen times twelve is a 'undred an' sixty-eight. Calcutta is the capital city o' West Bengal, an' 'as an established popperlation o' three million one 'undred an' forty-one thousand. Oo-ah!' he cried gleefully. 'It works, so it do, good as new!'

'I say!' same a thin voice, piercing his reverie. 'My man! You up there!'

The scarecrow ignored it, quite happy with all the knowledge inside his clever head.

'In a right-angled triangle the square on the 'ypo-tenuse is equal to the sum o' the squares on the other two sides, so 'tis.'

Miss Jamieson took a deep breath and shouted again. 'I say there! Do you hear me! You there! Tramp!'

Worzel Gummidge glanced down disdainfully.

'Don't interrupt me now, missus, I'm tryin' out me new 'ead.'

'None of your cheek!' she shrilled indignantly. 'I'll have you know that I'm a member of the teaching staff of this school, and I demand to know what you are doing up there. I shall require a *satisfactory answer!*' she piped.

The scarecrow grinned down at her, his new head

putting him in an uncommonly good mood. 'I'll give 'ee an answer, missus,' he beamed. 'I'll give 'ee as many answers as 'ee wants. Provided o' course, as I gets a satisfactory question first orf. Axe me a question about 'istory,' he suggested.

The schoolmistress looked rather put out.

'Don't be ridiculous!' she snapped.

Worzel Gummidge shrugged, not at all worried.

'The square root o' seven thousand four 'undred an' sixty-nine is ninety-seven,' he announced to no one in particular. 'The city o' Jo'annesburg were founded in eighteen sixty-six an' now 'as an estimated popperlation o' six 'undred an' fifty-five thousand.'

Miss Jamieson stamped her foot.

'Are you going to come down from there, *at once*, or am I to send for the policeman?' she demanded.

'I'll come down orl right, missus,' the scarecrow insisted, 'after you's axed me a question. Go on, axe me summat 'istorical.'

'Don't be ridiculous. I shall do no such thing.'

'Suit yourself. I'm stoppin' where I am.'

Realizing that the only way of shifting the strange figure on the roof was to go along with him, Miss Jamieson relented.

'Oh, all right,' she sighed wearily. 'Anything to put a stop to this nonsense. In what year did Queen Elizabeth the First ascend the throne?'

'Fifteen 'undred an' fifty-eight. Go on, axe me another.'

The schoolmistress's thick eyebrows lifted in surprise.

'Good heavens! Henry the Fifth?'

'Henry Five? Born thirteen eighty-seven. Came to the throne fourteen thirteen. Defeated them there froggies at Agincourt fourteen fifteen, an' died fourteen twenty-two. Axe me another!' he concluded triumphantly.

'This is *quite* unbelievable!' Miss Jamieson exclaimed.

'Go on,' encouraged Worzel Gummidge. 'Axe me another. Try me on summat else. Geography if you wants. I don't mind what it is. Geography, nuclear physics, shepherdin' sheep – anything as takes your fancy, missus.'

Miss Jamieson, despite herself, was quite intrigued.

'Name me the capital city of Australia.'

'Too easy, missus,' sighed the scarecrow. 'Canberra. Axe me another.'

'Er ... where is Timbuktu?'

'Central Mali, in Wessern Africa. Estimated popperlation, ten thousand. Thass not countin' scarecrows, o' course!'

The schoolmistress quivered with delight at her discovery.

'But this is absolutely incredible! I must inform the Headmaster of this! Stay there!' she fluttered. 'Don't go away. I shall be back anon.'

The scarecrow watched her hurry away across the playground.

'Daft ol' besom!' he growled. 'I ain't likely to go anywhere, am I? Not if I can't get down from off of this 'ere roof, I ain't.'

He noticed with a start that the ladder had reappeared a few yards closer to him that it was originally.

''Ello,' he decided. 'Looks like I can get down now, so it does,' and he inched his way towards it.

'Headmaster!' cried Miss Jamieson as she caught sight of Mr Foster emerging from his office, 'might I crave a moment of your valuable time?'

The Headmaster looked resignedly at the fluttering, fussing figure bearing down on him and sighed.

'If it *is* a moment, Miss Jamieson, and if it is *important*! I do have your own form for the next period of general knowledge, and I think you are already late for the gym class, are you not?'

'I'm sure you'll think it important, Headmaster,' she gushed, her thick spectacles steaming up, 'when I tell you that I have discovered a genius on the school roof!'

Mr Foster's eyebrows shot up like Venetian blinds.

'I *beg* your pardon, Miss Jamieson?'

'A *genius*, Headmaster,' she insisted. 'A brokendown tramp he may be, but he is a tramp who has obviously known *better times*. He has a remarkable brain, Headmaster, and he is sitting on the school roof, even as I speak to you.'

The Headmaster smiled benignly and patted his colleague's shoulder sympathetically.

'Miss Jamieson, I *know* about the man on the roof. He is no tramp. He's Mr Peters, the father of John and Sue, the new pupils. Mr Braithwaite recommended him. He's replacing the broken tiles.'

Miss Jamieson stood her ground.

'He was meant for far, far better things, Headmaster. Be he tramp or workman, it matters little. I can only repeat, Headmaster, that the man has a most remarkable brain. An I.Q. that is truly *phenomenal*.'

Mr Foster frowned. 'Are you *sure* of this, Miss Jamieson?' he asked, impressed by her stubbornness.

'He invited me to test him, Headmaster. I bombarded him with all manner of questions, and he answered every one. History, geography, mathematics – the man is an authority on every subject from nuclear physics to ... to ... sheep shearing!'

The Headmaster scratched his head.

'That may not necessarily be a sign of *genius*, Miss Jamieson,' he pointed out gently. 'Quite probably Mr Peters has a photographic mind. A good retentive memory. Still, if he's as good as you say he is –'

'Oh, *better*, Headmaster, *much* better,' she insisted.

The Headmaster made up his mind.

'Thank you, Miss Jamieson. I shall deal with this. Now: you don't want to be late for your gym class, do you?' and he strode away down the corridor, leaving the flushed Miss Jamieson to go and change into her shorts.

'How deeeeep is the oceeeean,' sang Mr Peters happily as he beavered away on the school roof, levering up old, broken tiles and carefully replacing them with new ones.

The scarecrow had rattled down the ladder while he'd been away collecting his bag of tools from the back of the car, and had slipped away across the playground, out through the gate, up the lane and out of the village without being spotted, and Mr Peters had taken his place on the roof a few minutes later without anyone being any the wiser.

'How high is the skyeeeeee?' he went on, 'How far is a journeyyyyyyyy from here to –'

'I say! Excuse me? Mr Peters?'

Mr Peters stopped in mid-verse and peered down into the playground to see the portly figure of the Headmaster gazing up at him.

'Come down a moment, would you, Mr Peters?'

'*Down*, Mr Foster?' he replied, puzzled.

'If you would be so kind, yes, please.'

He gesticulated at the roof.

'But I haven't finished these tiles yet!'

'Never mind the tiles!' fussed the Headmaster impatiently. 'I have another little task for you. And one I think will be *much* better suited to your natural talents.'

Mr Peters clambered down the ladder, puzzled but interested.

'Is it electrical work, Mr Foster?' he asked curiously.

'You'll see, you'll see!' beamed the tubby little Headmaster, 'Kindly follow me,' and he led the way importantly into the school.

As the Headmaster entered, the children stopped talking and fighting and shouting and came quickly to order, looking curiously at Mr Peters standing awkwardly behind him.

'Settle down, children,' Mr Foster beamed. 'Pay

attention. I have a surprise for you this afternoon. But first of all I'd like you to say good afternoon to Mr Peters.'

'Good afternoon, Mr Peters,' they chorused dutifully.

He clutched his cap in front of him and looked uncomfortable.

''Ow do, kids,' he muttered.

'Now then,' the Headmaster went on. 'General knowledge. And this afternoon, for a change, I am going to sit back and let you ask the questions. And Mr Peters here is going to give us all the answers!'

'What?' squeaked Mr Peters in alarm, for he'd never been much of a brain when he was at school, though he'd always been good with his hands.

John and Sue, who knew that perfectly well, exchanged a horrified glance.

'Crikey!' whispered Sue, sinking down as if she hoped the seat would swallow her.

'Crikey *Moses!*' agreed John, following her down.

'Mr Peters is an expert on general knowledge. Right, Mr Peters?' asked Mr Foster.

Mr Peters floundered, glancing at the door as if he was wondering whether to make a dash for it.

'Well, I wouldn't go so far as to say that –' he muttered.

The Headmaster chuckled. 'Come now, come now! No false modesty! Mr Peters, children, has a photographic memory. He can answer questions on any subject under the sun, and possibly *about* the sun, eh, Mr Peters?'

Mr Peters looked miserable. '*Me*, Mr Foster?'

John and Sue looked embarrassed and wished they were somewhere else.

The Headmaster decided to set the ball rolling.

'Now!' he cried. 'First question – an easy one for starters, ha ha! In what year did Columbus discover America?'

At that moment, Mr Peters wished that Columbus had never even heard of America!

'Er ... Ten sixty-six, was it?' he guessed hopelessly, dredging up the only date he could remember.

The Headmaster chortled.

'Ha ha! Very funny! Serves me right for asking such a simple question, eh?'

Outside, Worzel Gummidge, who had come back to collect his workaday head from the rooftop, pricked up his ears at the sound of the word 'question' and peered in through the window as he climbed down the ladder.

'Now seriously,' the Headmaster continued, 'what are the principal exports of Thailand?'

As Mr Peters shuffled uncomfortably from foot to foot, his mind a complete blank, the scarecrow mouthed the answer through the window, though no one could hear.

Mr Foster frowned.

John and Sue caught one another's eyes while their father ummed and erred.

'Shall we rescue him?' whispered John.

'I think we've *got* to,' his sister replied urgently.

John took a deep breath, raised his hand and called: 'I've got a question! Who won the Cup Final in nineteen fifty-three?'

As quick as a computer, Mr Peters rattled off the

answer with a happy smile – this was something he *did* know the answer to!

'Blackpool beat Bolton Wanderers, four three. Stanley Mortensen got a hat trick for Blackpool and Stanley Matthews got his first Cup Winners' Medal.'

The children were impressed. From the front row a fat, spotty boy called out.

'Who won the World Cup in nineteen sixty-two?'

Mr Peters' grin widened. These were easy!

'The World Cup in nineteen sixty-two was played in Chile and in the final Brazil beat Czechoslovakia by three goals to one.'

Another boy stuck up his hand.

'Who were the Football League champions in the season nineteen sixty-eight to sixty-nine?'

'Leeds United. Liverpool were the runners up.'

There was a round of applause from the children. The scarecrow, not much interested in football, finished climbing down the ladder and wandered away with his workaday head under his arm.

Mr Foster frowned – this wasn't quite the sort of general knowledge he'd had in mind.

'Yes,' he said. 'Very good, but I don't think we want *all* the questions to be about football, do we? Can someone give us another subject?'

John glanced at Sue and nodded.

She jumped to her feet.

'Which horse won the Grand National in nineteen sixty-four?'

Mr Peters smiled smugly, took a deep breath, and answered; 'Team Spirit, owned by J. Goodman, trained

by Fulke Walwyn, ridden by Willie Robinson. Came
in at eighteen to one.'

The room erupted to thunderous applause from the
children and Mr Foster realized that there was no
stopping them as they bombarded the happy Mr Peters
with strings of sporting questions. General knowledge
was the most successful lesson of the day!

In the afternoon, on their way home from school, as
the sun was fading into a sullen burning ball over the
hill, the children jumped the stile and skipped across
the field to visit the scarecrow, back on duty on his
pole.

'Hello, Worzel,' cried Sue cheerfully as he opened
one baleful eye to stare at them.

'What happened then, Worzel? Did you find your
clever head?' asked John.

''Ello, you three kids,' the scarecrow croaked.

John shook his head. 'He didn't find it.'

The scarecrow sneered. 'That's 'ow much you know,
mister clever clogs, 'cos I did find it, see. An' I've 'ad
it on.'

Sue gazed at him. 'Did it know a lot of things,
Worzel?'

The scarecrow's face became quite pompous.

'That there 'ead, my gal, knows everything there is
to be knowed. As a matter o' fact,' he said, wriggling
uncomfortably, 'that there 'ead knows a sight too
much.'

'Where is it?' Sue asked.

''Id!' said Worzel Gummidge firmly. 'I 'ad to get

rid o' it. Fair gave me 'eadache it did. Spoutin' all them facts and figures.'

'It couldn't give *you* a headache,' argued John logically, his head cocked on one side, 'it could only do that to itself.'

The scarecrow sneered again, curling his lip at the boy.

'You'm not so danged smart, young feller-me-lad. 'Cos as it 'appens, it gave me stummick a 'eadache. Little robin redbreast's 'ead's whirlin' round an' round still.'

Sue frowned. 'So where did you hide it this time, Worzel?'

Worzel Gummidge shrugged indifferently.

'Somewhere's safe. Even I don't know where. Only that there clever 'ead knows where it's 'id isself. An' I ain't goin' lookin' for it never again, so I ain't. For all I cares, wherever it's 'id, it's *stoppin'* 'id!'

At the end of the day, when the world was dark and still under the moonless sky and the children were sound asleep, Mr Braithwaite and Harry, dog-tired from working all day on the farm, were winding things up in the cowshed, doing the books.

'And how many gallons have we had so far this week, Harry?' asked the farmer wearily.

'Let's see now. We 'ad thirty-six gallons Sunday, thirty-five Monday, thirty-seven yesterday, an' another thirty-six today, Mister Braithwaite.'

'Right. So what's that in toto, Harry?'

In the smelly darkness of the cowshed, Harry

frowned, and tried to count on his fingers. 'Well, er . . .'

From the black above his head, a voice drifted down.

' 'Undred an' forty-four,' it croaked.

'Er . . . hundered and forty-four gallons, Mr Braithwaite,' echoed Harry, looking round and looking puzzled.

Mr Braithwaite's voice drifted through the gloom from the other end of the cowshed.

'What's that in litres, Harry?'

'Six 'undred an' forty-five,' prompted the voice.

Harry stared around, the hairs on the back of his neck standing on end.

'Six hundred and forty-five, Mr Braithwaite,' he called, his voice quavering a little.

'Thanks, Harry. Good night.' called Mr Braithwaite as he left the silent cowshed.

Harry shuffled round, peering into the darkness.

' 'Ere? Who said that?' he whispered fearfully.

There was a hint of a ghostly chuckle.

Harry fled.

On one of the beams, high above his head, a sacking-wrapped parcel muttered to itself . . .

CHAPTER 5
The Scarecrow Wedding

THE weather, always perverse, changed again, and a final fortnight of bright sunshine held back the early autumn mists just a little longer. In the orchard the plums were fat and shiny, purple and yellow, and huge clusters of apples dragged down the branches of the trees. There were pies at that time in Mrs Braithwaite's ever-open kitchen; apple and rhubarb and plum, all juicy and sweet, with crisp pastry crusts.

'I could do with some blackberries, mind,' the farmer's wife announced one morning as Sue stood helping her with her baking. 'There's nothing in all the world as nice as a new-made pie full of apples off of your own tree and blackberries wild from the hedgerow, so if you two youngsters want to take a couple of those big baskets down to Foggy Bottom—'

Sue had dusted the flour from her hands and was out of the kitchen almost before the red-cheeked woman had finished speaking.

'Super idea, Mrs Braithwaite,' she called over her shoulder. 'We shan't be long.'

In the caravan, where he had been curled up on the window seat with a pair of field-glasses, watching a kestrel sweeping the edge of the woods in lazy circles, John admitted that it wasn't a bad idea, at that.

'Do you remember how we used to read about things

like that?' he asked. 'You know, blackberrying, and birdwatching, and things. When we used to live in town?'

Sue unbuttoned her loose cotton frock and hung it carefully away in the narrow little wardrobe.

'And now we can do it whenever we like,' she nodded. 'I think I'll wear my dungarees,' she said thoughtfully, 'so that I don't get scratched. Are you going to change?'

John slid off the window seat and pulled on his own dungarees, and in a few minutes they were away, running across the fields towards the thick, tangled hedges that bounded the woods by Foggy Bottom, carrying two of Mrs Braithwaite's deep wicker baskets, and in half an hour were engrossed in their task, their mouths rimmed with purple.

As the children made their slow way home in the heat of the middle of the day, Worzel Gummidge set off for a stroll, bored with standing in one place all the time. He left Ten-acre Field by the stile and headed for the village, making a short detour to grub up some crunchy rhubarb to munch along the way. Near Scatterbrook Farm, he paused.

'How do, pusscat,' he called cheerily to a sunbathing tabby, stretched out along a wall. 'Caught any mouses lately?' He shook his head. 'Don't know why for I's talkin' to 'im. 'E can't talk back. Too stewpid, so 'e is.'

As he turned away, there was the sound of a squeaky little voice.

'Help!'

The scarecrow turned back and frowned at the cat. 'Parding?' he asked in surprise.

'Help!' came the squeak again.

The scarecrow scratched his head and then, since it was a nice, fine morning, scratched the cat's as well.

'Help what, eh? Help you catch mouses? You catch your own mouses! You don't never catch no rooks for ol' Worzel, does you?'

There was another squeak, louder this time.

'Help! Up here!'

The scarecrow spun round three times and ended up staring across the lane into the air where, high up in the branches of a conker-laden chestnut tree, hung Aunt Sally, suspended by her ankles.

'Well,' he gasped, waddling over to stand underneath and look up at her. 'Clot my 'ead an' turn it into butter! If it ain't Aunt Sally! What you a'doin' of up that there tree then, Aunt Sally?'

'I was thrown here by a bull!' she whimpered.

Worzel Gummidge nodded. 'Ar! Nasty, brutish beast, that there bull is. I knows it of old. That's why I sticks to the lane, same as like what you should'a done, Aunt Sally,' he said unhelpfully.

High above his head, Aunt Sally wriggled dangerously. 'Don't just stand there chattering, you stupid scarecrow! Get me down!'

He looked up at her and shook his head. 'Ar. That's easier said nor what it's done. Oo-ah.'

'There is a *ladder* in the *barn*,' she squeaked desperately.

Worzel Gummidge squinted up at her. The high

midday sun was in his eyes. 'The barn, eh?' he asked thoughtfully. 'What barn would that be, then?'

Aunt Sally stormed at him. 'The *barn* in the *field*!'

The scarecrow didn't move. 'The field, eh? What field?'

'The *field* on the other side of the *wall*, you half-witted turnip!'

Worzel Gummidge shook his head. ''Alf-witted I may be, Aunt Sally, but barmy I ain't. That bull be in that there field, bain't 'e?'

Aunt Sally wheedled. 'What if he is? Don't tell me you're *afraid*!'

'What?' laughed the scarecrow, 'Ol' Worzel? Afraid o' a bull?' He stopped laughing, shook his head firmly and set off down the lane. 'I'll go fetch the Crowman.'

'Come back here, you coward!' Aunt Sally screamed.

He slowly turned and looked up at her. 'I ain't no coward, Aunt Sally, it's just that I's got the wrong 'ead on for tacklin' bulls. You just wait till I gets 'old o' a Bull-Tacklin' 'Ead! Oo-ah!'

He turned away again, calling over his shoulder as he went. 'Don't go away, mind!'

He heard a sob, and his pace slowed.

The sob turned into a snivel, then into a wail, and very slowly, with great reluctance, he retraced his steps, his lip quivering and his eyes moist.

'Now don't you start that blubberin' an' snivellin' an' weepin'. You know what'll happen: you'll set me off a blubberin' an' a-snivellin' an' a-weepin' an' then we'll be 'ere all day! You up the tree an' me down it!'

'Then don't leave me, Worzel!' Aunt Sally wailed piteously.

The scarecrow's beady eyes lit up. 'If that's what you wants, Aunt Sally, I'll stay 'ere for ever an' ever, so I will. But you don't get me tanglin' with that there tarnation bull.'

'Not even if I ask you nicely?' she pleaded.

'Not even if you axes me as nice as treacle pudden,' said Worzel Gummidge firmly.

'Not even if I promise to ... to *marry* you?' she squeaked breathlessly.

Worzel Gummidge's jaw dropped. 'Promise to *marry* me?' His eyes suddenly narrowed and his mouth set sullenly. 'You's 'avin' ol' Worzel on. You shouldn't mock a pore ol' scarecrow, Aunt Sally. Shame on you.'

Aunt Sally took a deep breath. 'Worzel Gummidge. Fetch that ladder and I will be your bride. May I get death-watch beetle in my pretty elbows if I tell a lie.'

'Well, chuck my best 'ead to the pigs! I thinks you means it!'

'I *do* mean it!' she insisted.

'Promise?' he asked, almost convinced.

'Promise, promise, promise!' she squealed. 'But hurry!'

The scarecrow gave in. 'I will that, m'dear,' he cried eagerly, 'bull or no bull!' With his lumbering, waddling walk he moved rapidly down the lane to the strong five-barred gate that led into the field where the bull lived, and levered it open. The bull heard the squeak of the gate and slowly turned its massive head. In the distance it saw a scarecrow, stock-still, its arms outspread on either side. Satisfied, the bull went on chewing the cud.

The scarecrow came to life again and crept towards the barn. Under his feet, a startled brace of partridges rose on clattering wings and whirred away. The bull turned again, more quickly this time, but once again saw only a motionless scarecrow on duty. The bull frowned. Surely that scarecrow wasn't in the same place? it wondered. But nothing was moving, so it went back to a particularly succulent piece of grass . . .

Worzel Gummidge's eyes swivelled: the bull had its massive hindquarters towards him again. He unfroze and crept quickly into the barn. A moment passed. The partridges circled the field and whirred in to land again. Worzel Gummidge's turnippy head appeared round the corner of the barn, spying out the lie of the land. He saw it was all clear, emerged carrying the ladder, and made for the gate as fast as his broomstick legs would carry him.

He paused to look at the notice on the gate. BEWARE OF THE BULL, it read. He sniffed. Without his reading head it didn't mean a thing. 'Whassat say?' he wondered. 'Please shut the gate? Why for should I? What's that there gate ever done for me?' and he strode out into the lane, leaving it open behind him.

Behind him, the bull caught sight of the open gate and began to amble lazily towards it . . .

'Hurry, Worzel!' called Aunt Sally from her perch in the tree.

He quickened his pace and leaned the ladder against the tree.

It was a trickier business than he'd expected: the ladder kept slipping this way and that, and by the time he'd managed to steady it against a thick branch his hat had fallen into the dust and he'd trodden on it several times. 'Dang blitherin' thing!' he shouted at the recalcitrant ladder. 'Worse nor a bloomin' scarecrow pole, so y'are, an' that's sayin' summat!'

'Do *hurry*, you stupid bag of straw!' screamed Aunt Sally.

The bull lumbered out into the lane, unseen by either of them, and began to paw the ground aggressively.

'Shan't be a jiffy, Aunt Sally. Got to put my 'at on,' he called, squinting up at her, 'Can't go climbin' trees with no 'at. I'd catch my death o' cold.'

He bent down to pick it up, his back to the snorting bull...

Approaching the farm with their baskets full of plump blackberries and their faces and hands purple with sweet juice, the children noticed that the scarecrow was absent from his pole, yet again.

'I wonder where Worzel's got to today?' said Sue.

John pulled a disapproving face. 'Up to no good wherever he is,' he suggested cynically.

His sister grinned at him and skipped away across the field. 'How do *you* know he's up to no good,' she called. 'You sound like somebody's grandad!'

There was a roaring, croaking scream. The children stopped dead in their tracks and stared into the sky as the figure of the scarecrow, arms outstretched, sailed through the air.

'Wasn't *that* Worzel?' asked Sue in a matter-of-fact sort of voice.

Her brother nodded. 'Well done, Worzel. He's obviously learnt to fly.'

By the time the children reached the spot where the huge chestnut tree hung over the lane, the bull had got bored with wandering in the dusty lane and had strolled back into the field in search of another few mouthfuls of grass.

'Good thing too,' observed John as he pulled the gate shut. 'Otherwise we'd end up joining *them* up there.'

High above their heads, Worzel Gummidge was perched on a branch of his own, looking very discomfited, not far from where Aunt Sally, still suspended by her ankles, was drumming her fingers impatiently on the tree trunk and muttering to herself.

'*Stupid* scarecrow!' she hissed, as the children set up the ladder again and helped them down, 'Stupid, iggerant, turnip-headed bag of straw!'

When they'd delivered their baskets of blackberries to Mrs Braithwaite the children decided to take Worzel Gummidge and Aunt Sally, rescued from their nesting places in the tree, into the village for tea and cakes, and in the cool of the afternoon they sat at little round tables outside the tiny tea shop.

'My my my,' exclaimed the scarecrow as Sue came out with a tray laden with bottles of lemonade and slices of cake. 'Fizzy pop an' a slice o' cake, slice o' cake an' fizzy pop! If this ain't my lucky day!' He licked his lips, then frowned as Sue set down the tray. 'This 'ere ain't chocklit cake,' he grumbled petulantly. 'I axed pertickeler for chocklit cake!'

Sue stamped her foot, and looked about to burst into tears. 'Don't be so ungrateful! I've spent all my pocket-money on this!'

Aunt Sally leaned over the table to her and put on her toffee-nosed voice. 'You'll have to . . . *H*excuse him. He hasn't got no manners.' She turned to the scarecrow and grabbed his slice of cake. 'If you don't want your cake, *aye'll* 'ave it!'

Worzel Gummidge immediately grabbed it back. 'Oh no you don't!' he croaked.

'Oh yes I do!' she squeaked, grabbing it back again and knocking over a bottle of lemonade in the process.

'Give that back 'ere!'

'Shan't!'

'It's mine!'

'Mine!' they shouted, as the cake went from hand to hand, crumbling away to crumbs. Bottles toppled and plates flew in the squabble, and a waitress came hurrying out of the little tea shop to see what all the noise was about.

'Well!' she said indignantly, her hands on her hips. She wagged a finger at Worzel Gummidge and Aunt Sally. 'If you can't keep these children in order you should leave them at home!' and she flounced back into the tea shop.

'I like that!' said John, feeling hard-done-by.

'You shut your 'ead an' go an' get some more cake!' snapped the scarecrow.

'With cream!' Aunt Sally specified.

'An' *chocklit*!' added the scarecrow fiercely.

John looked aghast at his sister, who shrugged her shoulders, feeling very hurt by all the rudeness. 'Go on, then, you can spend *your* pocket-money for a change.'

'Why should I?'

Worzel Gummidge answered for Sue. ''Cos you's the only one whose pockets 'as *got* money, that's why for. I's got pockets but they ain't got no money 'cos 'e won't give me no wages, so 'e won't. So go an' get us that there slice o' cake, or I'll sit 'ere an' sulk till to-morrer cockcrow.'

Aunt Sally laid her thin little hand on his thigh and smiled sweetly. 'And if you don't, I'll jab you with my hatpin!' she said cruelly.

Sue sighed. 'Oh, go on, John. I'll pay you back out of my piggy bank.'

'You'd *better*,' he answered threateningly, going back into the tea shop.

The scarecrow beamed ingratiatingly at Sue. 'What a nice little woman you is, missy! There orter be more yewmans likes o' you, so there ought. An' because you's so nice an' kind, ol' Worzel's going to let you into a secret. Her an' me's gettin' married.'

'Oh no we ain't!' said Aunt Sally sniffily.

The scarecrow scowled. 'Oh yes we is, you double-crossin' broom'andle. You promised!'

'I did no such thing!' she lied. 'Marry you? *I'm* going to marry a Duke from Rumania, else Egypt. Not a flippin' 'ayrick!'

Worzel Gummidge's eyes flooded with tears as he

turned to Sue. 'It were a different story when she were up that there ol' tree, missy! Promise, promise, promise, sez she! Fetch that there ladder an' I'll be your bride, sez she!'

'But that was when I was up a tree, you stupid scarecrow!' she sneered. 'I'm not up a tree now, am I?'

'But you can't go back on a *promise*, Aunt Sally,' said Sue.

She stuck her nose in the air. 'Of course I can, you stupid little girl. I can do whatever I please.'

The scarecrow looked crestfallen. 'Crool, that's what you is. Crool an' vicious an' mean. I 'opes you gets woodworm.'

There was a sly glint in Sue's eye as she spoke. 'Never mind, Worzel. You can always marry a lady scarecrow like Earthy Mangold.'

'*If* she'll have him,' sneered Aunt Sally.

'She'll have him tomorrow if he asks her –' said Sue glibly, 'especially when she sees the wedding dress.'

'Wedding dress? What wedding dress?' snapped Aunt Sally, her eyes gleaming.

'The one my Dad got from a jumble sale. For my dressing-up box,' Sue replied airily. 'It's white brocade with a mandarin collar, lace sleeves and a *beautiful* long train.'

Aunt Sally was entranced! 'Lace sleeves and a beautiful long train,' she breathed. 'Tell me, little girl, does it have a veal?'

Sue frowned. 'A *veal* ... Oh! You mean a veil! Yes, of course!'

'A veil!' squealed Aunt Sally, 'A veil for my pretty face! Oh, Worzel, name the day!'

Worzel Gummidge frowned. 'Don't rightly know, Aunt Sally. Sat'dy I think.'

'Not today!' she shouted, slapping the table. 'The day for our wedding, you oafish turnip!'

The scarecrow gasped. 'Our wedding? Does you mean it?' He turned to Sue for reassurance. 'Does she mean it, missy?'

Bright-eyed, and a bit smug at the way her plotting had worked, Sue nodded vigorously. 'Aunt Sally,' said Worzel, as John came out of the tea shop with another tray of lemonade and cake, 'You's made me the 'appiest scarecrow this side o' Foggy Bottom. You'll never regret it, not never. I'll work for you an' make a 'ome for you an' you'll never want for nothin'!'

He eyed the cakes on the table greedily and licked his lips. 'An' I'll just 'ave your piece o' cake 'cos it's bigger nor mine, see?'

Aunt Sally leapt to her feet and grabbed the cake back again. 'Give that back, you greedy horsehair mattress!'

''Tain't me what's greedy, you bloomin' walkin' clothespeg! 'Tis you! When we gets married you'll 'ave dry bread to eat an' you won't 'ave nothin' else!'

Aunt Sally leered. 'Oh yes I shall! I shall put your stupid head in a pot and have vegetable stew!'

As they began to grab at one another's cakes and to hurl crumbs and insults at each other there came the soft tinkle of a cowbell, and they froze as the Crowman swung slowly round the corner and pulled up beside them.

The scarecrow whipped out a grubby handkerchief and vigorously dusted off a seat for the Crowman.

'Why, Mr Crowman, sir, welcome to our 'umble table, an' please to 'ave a seat an' a slice o' cake ... An' 'ow ever did your 'igh an' mightiness know as we was 'ere?'

The Crowman sat down. His clear eyes looked deep into the scarecrow's, and Worzel Gummidge shifted uneasily.

'A little bird told me, Worzel,' he said softly, fishing out a robin from his waistcoat pocket.

Worzel Gummidge took it and looked closely at it. 'That gossipy little b ... bird! Well, robin redbreast? 'As you been an' gone an' blabbed it all out about me an' 'er gettin' wed?'

'Is it true, Aunt Sally?' asked the Crowman.

'Oh, indeed it *is*, Mr Crowman,' she gushed. 'And I'm to wear a white brocade gown with a mandarin collar, lace sleeves and a beautiful long train. And a veil. What is being specially made by my dressmaker,' she elaborated as her imagination ran away with her.

The scarecrow leaned forward across the table and touched his hat respectfully to the Crowman.

'Ar. I've got an important question to axe, Mr Crowman, your worship. Is it right that when you 'as a weddin', you 'as a weddin' cake?'

The Crowman held Worzel Gummidge's eyes as he leaned forward. 'First things first, Worzel. *I've* got an even more important question to ask you. Do you really want to go through with this marriage?'

The scarecrow nodded so hard that he loosened his head, and had to screw it down tight before he could reply. 'With all my 'eart an' straw, your eminence.'

'Even though you weren't made for each other?'

''Umbly beggin' your parding, Mr Crowman, sir, but we was.'

'But you were *not*!' said the Crowman, so sharply that he startled the scarecrow. '*I* made you, Worzel. I didn't make Aunt Sally.'

Aunt Sally preened. 'Of course not. *Aye* happen to have been made by a fully trained wood-carver.'

'Even so, your honour, Mr Crowman, sir,' interjected the scarecrow, 'she'll do for me.'

The Crowman sighed, stood up, and replaced his tall black hat. 'Very well,' he decided. 'I'll put up the scarecrow banns!'

The days passed, and the Indian summer faded into a golden autumnal glow. The swifts and swallows went home for the winter, and tawny owls began to call in the late afternoon mist, flopping slowly over the farm on broad white wings in search of rats and mice in the hayricks and barns.

In the farmyard one morning, as they lugged a heavy bucket of pig-swill out to the sty, Mr Peters and Mr Braithwaite paused to examine an odd device perched on the gatepost. On top of a neat pyramid of woven hawthorn twigs, a single bent hazel twig pointed like an arrow across the fields.

'What do you make of that, Mr Peters?' asked the farmer.

They put down their bucket. Mr Peters took off his

cloth cap and scratched his head. 'Search me, Mr Braithwaite. Don't gypsies leave signs like that? Or so I've heard.'

Mr Braithwaite shook his head; he'd seen gypsy signs often enough in the past, but he didn't recognize the scarecrow banns. 'Not gypsies, Mr Peters. There's been no gypsies round here for donkey's years. Besides, that's not a Romany sign.'

Mr Peters looked blank. 'Oh no. No,' he muttered, 'I can tell it's not a *Romany* sign. Do you reckon it means something?'

The farmer shrugged. 'I don't know whether it does or not. All I know is, that's the fifth one I've seen hereabouts in the last fortnight,' and they picked up the bucket and headed for the pigs.

Outside the farmhouse, near the little kitchen garden, Mrs Braithwaite paused in hanging out her washing and raised her eyebrows at the sight of John and Sue, emerging from the caravan dressed in their best clothes. 'Hello?' she asked in surprise. 'Where are you off to, all dressed up to the nines?'

They looked guiltily at one another. 'To a birthday party,' said Sue, just as John said, 'To a wedding.'

'Well?' laughed the farmer's wife. 'Which is it? A wedding or a birthday party?'

'A wedding!' said Sue, trying to agree with John, at the very moment that John, trying to agree with Sue, cried out, 'A birthday party!'

The children felt hopelessly confused, but the plump, jolly woman was laughing and shaking her head as her husband and Mr Peters appeared lugging their empty bucket. 'I think you're having me on!' she said, 'I was just saying, Mr Peters, they're all dressed up but they don't seem to know where they're going!'

The farmer put down the bucket and lit his pipe. 'Sunday School treat, isn't it?' he said.

Mr Peters looked puzzled. 'Sunday School treat? I thought you were going to tea at Mrs Bloomsbury-Barton's?'

Mrs Braithwaite shook her head and chuckled again. 'A wedding, they cracked on to me they were going to.'

'*Whose* wedding?' their father asked. He couldn't think of anyone who was getting married.

'Or a birthday party,' the farmer's wife added.

'*What* birthday party?' said Mr Peters, quite hopelessly confused by now.

Sue crossed her fingers. 'It was a joke.'

'Funny sort of joke,' her father observed dourly.

'Jokes are *supposed* to be funny,' John pointed out cheekily.

His father wagged a finger at him. 'You watch your step.' He turned to his daughter. 'And what have you got behind your back?'

She shook her head. 'Nothing.'

'Come on, then,' Mr Peters insisted. 'Let's have a look at nothing.'

Reluctantly, Sue brought out her hands from behind her back, and showed a bunch of flowers.

'My pansies!' exclaimed Mrs Braithwaite.

She shook her head. 'They might *look* like your

pansies, Mrs Braithwaite. But they're not *really* your pansies. It's a posy.'

'Right!' said Mr Peters suddenly. 'We'll get to the bottom of this! *What* are you two doing, wearing your best clothes, with a bunch of Mrs Braithwaite's flowers?'

Sue took a deep breath. 'We're going to a hedge-hog's funeral, if you *really* want to know.'

The adults looked amazed, then suddenly burst out laughing all together.

'A hedgehog's funeral!' cried Mrs Braithwaite as the children hurried out through the gate and away across the field. 'Bless their little hearts! Go on then. And don't be late for tea!'

Across the fields towards the woods, the morning mist seemed somehow thicker, whirling like a living thing, yet not at all cold. High on a hill overlooking the woods, there was another sign like the one on the farmer's gatepost, but this one was huge, a massive pyramid of tree branches with the long, straight trunk of a young elm pointing towards the woods.

Out of the swirling mist, singly, and in pairs and in groups, scarecrows emerged like ghosts, heading for the woods, the mist opening and closing behind them. Down the hill and into the trees they marched, Sarah Tater, Hannah Harrow, Soggy Boggart, Upsadaisy, following the secret paths that led to the Crowman's house.

Outside the house, Sergeant Beetroot was in charge, striding up and down with his hazel swagger-stick, marshalling the guests into their proper places, clouting Worzel Gummidge's nephew, Pickles, whenever he reached for his catapult, bowing low to Earthy Mangold and Saucy Nancy, and looking disapprovingly at Worzel Gummidge's long-lost cousin, Cobber, who'd come all the way from Australia for the wedding.

'Ever so exciting, isn't it?' cooed Saucy Nancy to Sergeant Beetroot. She'd had a new coat of varnish and her hair was braided with seaweed. 'I've never been to a scarecrow wedding before. You landlubbers have all the fun!'

Sergeant Beetroot's celery moustache bristled as he spotted Saucy Nancy winking at Cousin Cobber. 'It's not fun, marm,' he barked, 'it's a solemn ceremony. An' I'll thank you to stop winking at the other guests.'

'I can't help myself, dearie,' she confessed with a broad grin. 'He's ever so handsome, ain't he? Who is it?'

'That's Worzel's cousin, Cobber, from Australey,' replied Sergeant Beetroot in a sniffy sort of voice. 'Stowed away on a grain ship, so he did, when he was a lad. Come back lately the same way.'

Saucy Nancy was entranced. 'Australey! Fancy that! He's got the sea in his blood, then, same as what I have.'

As Saucy Nancy and Cousin Cobber ogled one another, Sergeant Beetroot went among the guests, distributing massive rhododendron buttonholes from a battered old seed tray. The Crowman's clear voice came down to the guests. 'Any sign of the bride and groom, Sergeant Beetroot?'

The scarecrow snapped to attention and gave a quivering salute. High above his head, on the balcony of the pigeon loft on the corner of his house, the Crowman was leaning over and looking down. There was a fresh, glossy crow feather in the band of his shiny black hat.

'I'll have a recce, sah!' barked the scarecrow. He nudged Saucy Nancy. 'Let me have your spy-glass, gel! Come along, come along, make it snappy!' he barked, and seizing the brass-bound telescope he scanned the margins of the trees through the mist.

He gave the Crowman a thumbs-up sign, and the Crowman nodded thoughtfully and went indoors.

Through the woods came a strange procession. First, led by Sue in her best frock, a mangy old donkey hauled a cart, and on the cart, on a rickety kitchen chair, Aunt Sally sat erect, very proud of herself in her tattered old once-white wedding dress.

Behind the donkey cart came Worzel Gummidge. His carriage was rather less impressive – a wheelbarrow, pushed by John – but from somewhere he'd managed to acquire a moth-eaten old morning suit, complete with spats and a grey top hat, and looked almost smart.

Sergeant Beetroot marched to the edge of the clearing, turned smartly on his heel, and called the company to order. 'Scarecrow hescort ... wait for it! Scarecrow hescort, atten-SHUN!'

The scarecrows shuffled and lurched into two ragged lines leading through the clearing to the Crowman's house, and from the balcony window came the strains of a harmonium.

Sue helped Aunt Sally carefully down from the cart, and John dumped Worzel Gummidge out of the wheelbarrow on to the grass in an unceremonious, undignified heap.

As the scarecrow collected himself, scowling at John, the two children picked up Aunt Sally's train and followed her slowly forwards.

'Scarecrow hescort ... humbrellys HUP!' barked Sergeant Beetroot, and Aunt Sally marched with dignity under the arched umbrellas into the Crowman's house.

Behind her, with a lot less dignity, Worzel Gummidge chatted with the guests, Sergeant Beetroot following behind to give them a parade-ground inspection.

'Arternoon, Saucy Nancy,' he beamed. 'Arternoon, Soggy Boggart. Nice of 'ee to come, Earthy Mangold – 'ave 'ee brought me a prezzie? 'Cos if 'ee ain't, you gets no cake! Now then, young Pickles, is you goin' to be'ave yourself?'

Pickles gave a sickly grin. 'Yes, Uncle Worzel.'

'You ain't brought your catapult?'

'No Uncle Worzel.'

''Cos if you knocks my 'ead off while I's gettin' married, you'll be for it!' and he belted the young scarecrow round the head, just to be on the safe side.

'AND get your straw cut, laddie!' Sergeant Beetroot hissed in his ear.

Worzel Gummidge spotted his long-lost cousin. 'My my my! If it ain't Cousin Cobber from Australey, turned up again like a bad penny.'

'Wotcher blue!' croaked the suntanned scarecrow. He wore a wide hat, with corks dangling on strings all round the brim.

'Wassamarrer then?' asked Worzel Gummidge. 'Didn't you like Australey?'

'Nothin' wrong with Australey, mate. They got rooks there the size o' flippin' horstrichies. I tell you, Bruce, a scarecrow can walk tall dahn under.'

'Pity you didn't stop there, then,' sniffed Worzel Gummidge.

'I would'a done, blue, only I drank too much ginger beer, crashed out in a grain elevator an' woke up on the 'igh seas. So I thought I'd come an' see you spliced, you ol' ratbag, before I hitch back to Wagga-Wagga.'

Worzel Gummidge's eyes gleamed. 'Fetched me anything back from Australey, 'ave 'ee?'

'Bar o' chocklit,' replied the other, making Worzel's mouth water. 'Only I et it.'

'You might as well'a stopped there, then,' said Worzel Gummidge sourly, moving on into the house.

Cousin Cobber grabbed Sergeant Beetroot's sleeve as he passed. ' 'Ere, 'oo's the Sheila?'

Sergeant Beetroot thought about it. 'What's it worth?' he asked out of the corner of his mouth.

'Bar o' chocklit?' suggested the Australian, producing one furtively.

Sergeant Beetroot pocketed it surreptitiously. 'Saucy Nancy,' he whispered, and started barking orders, ushering the other scarecrows into the house.

Indoors, the Crowman was playing odd little melodies on his harmonium, pumping away with his feet.

'Come along now, move yourselves, move yourselves,' barked Sergeant Beetroot. 'Bride next to the bridegroom, that's the idea.' He turned to John and Sue. 'You two yewmans sit at the back ... And where d'you think you're going, laddie?'

Pickles winced as Sergeant Beetroot belted his head. 'Fetch a slice o' cake sir!' he quavered.

'You'll get your cake after the wedding and not before! Now get yourself in line! Move!' Sergeant Beetroot stepped smartly forward and saluted the Crowman. 'All present and correct, sah!'

The Crowman struck up *The Scarecrow's Wedding March* on his harmonium, and the ragged line moved forward in a strange, eccentric dance, leaping and hopping, down the room to stand before a long table. The Crowman joined them and took his place on the far side of the table.

'Are you Worzel Hedgerow Gummidge?'

The Scarecrow frowned. 'What a funny question, your eminence, Mr Crowman, sir. You *knows* my name sir, seein' as 'ow you gave it me.'

The Crowman sighed. 'Just answer the question, Worzel. Are you Worzel Hedgerow Gummidge?'

'I am that, sir,' he beamed.

'And are you Aunt Roll Up Roll Up Three Balls A Penny Sally?' the Crowman continued.

'I am,' whispered Aunt Sally beneath her veil.

The Crowman raised his voice to speak to the whole company. 'Who giveth this Aunt Sally away?'

Aunt Sally jerked, and threw back her veil. 'Giveth me away? Giveth me away?' she squealed indignantly, 'Begging your pardon, Mr Crowman, for speaking so impertinent, but I'm far too precious to be giveth away. I'll have you know a fairground gentleman once offered five guineas for me, sight unseen!'

'Aunt Sally,' explained the Crowman patiently, 'if you're to marry Worzel, someone has to give you away!'

'Marry Worzel?' she sniffed. 'I'm not going to marry Worzel!'

The scarecrow leaned forward and spoke softly to the Crowman. 'She is, your worship, sir. She just says she ain't 'cos she's barmy.'

Pickles whipped out his catapult. 'Shall I knock her head off, Uncle Worzel? *Ow!*' he yelped as Worzel Gummidge belted him again.

The Crowman brought the proceedings to order. 'Aunt Sally, are you telling me you've changed your mind again?'

'Good heavens, *no*, Mr Crowman!' she explained with a patronizing smirk. '*Aye* never meant to marry that dirty old scarecrow in the first place. Aye'm *far* too grand. The whole idea's preposterous!'

The Crowman's eyes flashed fire, and the scarecrows shuffled fearfully. 'Then why, may I ask, have we called all these scarecrows together?' he hissed softly.

Aunt Sally preened herself. 'So they can admire me

in my beautiful wedding dress and I can have my beautiful photo took and be in all the papers.'

'Oh, Worzel,' said the Crowman to the crestfallen scarecrow, 'I did warn you!'

'Can't you *make* 'er marry me, sir?' begged the scarecrow abjectly. 'I worships the ground she stands on, Mr Crowman, sir! Couldn't you pull 'er legs off an' not give 'em back till we's man an' wife?'

The Crowman shook his head.

Cousin Cobber called out, 'Never you mind, blue. I reckon she's a right pain in the gizzard. I mean, just look at her! With a shape like that you could use 'er for roddin' out drains!'

Worzel Gummidge bridled. 'Don't you talk about my Aunt Sally like that, Cousin Cobber, or I'll knock your 'ead off!'

Pickles crept forward while Sergeant Beetroot was having a hurried consultation with some of the other scarecrows. 'Shall *I* knock his head off, Uncle Worzel? *Ow!*' he yelped, as the sharp-eared Sergeant clobbered him again.

'Permission to speak, sah!'

The Crowman nodded to Sergeant Beetroot. 'Yes, Sergeant?'

'Some of the scarecrows was wonderin', sah. If there ain't goin' to be no weddin', does they get any cake?'

The Crowman shook his head sadly. 'I'm afraid not. No wedding, no cake.'

Cousin Cobber groaned. 'Aw! There has to be a weddin'! I come thousands o' miles from Australey an' I'm not goin' back without my bit o' cake!'

Saucy Nancy fluttered her eyelashes at Worzel Gummidge. 'Well, shipmate, if there has to be a wedding and she won't take you on, *I* wouldn't mind having you aboard.'

The scarecrow was taken aback. 'Me? Never! You's too ugly.'

Cousin Cobber examined her speculatively. 'I don't know so much, Blue,' he mused, 'I've seen worse. Out in the bush.'

'Well *you* marry 'er then,' suggested Worzel Gummidge.

The Australian considered it. 'I wouldn't mind. Fancy travellin' the high seas back to Australey, mate?' he said to Saucy Nancy.

She fluttered her green eyelashes. 'The 'igh seas! Oh! Mr Crowman, sir,' she gasped, 'marry us this minute!'

The Crowman held up a warning hand. 'Now, Saucy Nancy, you must think what you're saying. Marrying Worzel's cousin would be almost as bad as marrying Worzel himself.'

Saucy Nancy shook her head stubbornly. 'I don't care, sir. To get back on the 'igh seas I'd ... I'd marry the ship's parrot! Oh, please Mr Crowman say you'll marry us!'

The Crowman smiled his slow, deep smile. 'I suppose if I didn't you'd still run away with him to Australia.'

'I would, sir, as fast as my wheels would carry me!'

'Then I'd better make an honest figurehead of you. And Worzel!' he called to the woebegone scarecrow.

'If you can stop blubbering for a moment, you can be Cobber's best scarecrow.'

Worzel Gummidge brightened visibly. 'Bestest scarecrow, sir? What do you think to that, Aunt Sally? Stewpid ol' Worzel's goin' to be the bestest scarecrow!'

Aunt Sally gave a derisory sniff and turned her back on him.

'Very well,' sighed the Crowman, 'let's get on with it. Are you Cobber Outback Gummidge?'

'I am that ...'

'And are you,' the Crowman continued in his mellifluous tones, 'The Figurehead of *The Saucy Nancy*, registered at Kingston-upon-Hull?'

'Aye aye, sir,' beamed the figurehead proudly.

'And who giveth this figurehead away?'

'*Give* her away?' murmured Aunt Sally, just loud enough for everyone to hear. 'I wouldn't even bother to *throw* her away!'

Sergeant Beetroot stepped smartly forward. 'I'll give her away. With the greatest of pleasure! Sah!'

'If any of you know of any reason why this scarecrow and this figurehead should not marry,' went on the Crowman soberly, 'Speak now or forever hold your peace. Did you speak, Worzel?'

'No sir, your honour, sir. I just snivelled,' admitted the scarecrow.

'Oh, *do* pull yourself together! Now ... Do you, Cobber Outback Gummidge, truly love this figurehead, Saucy Nancy?'

The scarecrow stood up straight and nodded firmly,

making the corks on his hat wobble. 'She'll do for me, blue,' he said, in a loud, proud voice.

'And do you, Saucy Nancy, truly love this scarecrow Cobber Outback Gummidge?'

She weighed him up with a seafarer's critical gaze, and nodded contentedly. 'I could go farther and fare worse, I reckon,' she admitted.

The Crowman was relieved that there seemed to be no more hitches.

'Repeat after me,' he instructed them.

They listened attentively, and the rest of the congregation hung on his words, spoken softly in the still air.

'I, Cobber Outback Gummidge ... do take thee, Saucy Nancy, as my wife ...'

The scarecrow dutifully echoed the Crowman's words as he spoke. 'In sunshine and in snow ... At seed-scattering time and in harvest ... in new clothes or old ...'

There was a reverent silence all over the room as the assembled scarecrows listened to the words, and there was a tear trickling down Worzel Gummidge's cheek as he mouthed the responses with his cousin Cobber, wishing that he and Aunt Sally could have been standing there.

'Through plague and pestilence, fire and water ... till both of us falls to pieces!' The Crowman turned to Saucy Nancy, proud and erect on her pram wheels. 'And now, Saucy Nancy,' he began, 'Repeat after me ... I, Saucy Nancy, do take thee ... Cobber Outback Gummidge as my husband ... in sunshine and in snow ...' As the awesome words rolled over the heads of the gathered scarecrows, Aunt Sally was miles away, in a world of her own, her eyes tight shut.

'I Aunt Sally,' she dreamed, 'do take thee, the Archduke of Rumania, Bulgaria and most of Egypt as my husband ... in sunshine and in snow ... with crowns and jewels ... with diamonds and with rubies ...'

At the climax of the ceremony, the Crowman lifted high over his head a basket of fruit and berries and corn. As he spoke, he slowly lowered it towards the bride and groom, who solemnly laid their hands on it.

'Apples for health,' he intoned, 'Corn for plenty, berries for happiness ... By the wind and the rain and all the seasons, I pronounce thee scarecrow and wife ...'

There was a ripple of irreverent but heartfelt applause around the room as the bride and groom kissed. Worzel Gummidge's hand crept towards Aunt Sally's and she, lost in her daydreams, took it for a moment, before waking up and shaking him off with a shudder.

The scarecrow's face crumpled, but the Crowman leaned over to cheer him. 'Cheer up, Worzel,' he murmured. 'And you too, Aunt Sally. Your part of the ceremony is only just beginning.'

The scarecrow looked puzzled. 'Our part of the cere ... cemerony ... this 'ere weddin' business? What's it got to do with us, sir? Might as well chuck us in the dustbin right now, so you might.'

Aunt Sally turned and looked at him sharply. 'Speak for yourself. Has our part of the ceremony got anything to do with *cake*, Mr Crowman?' she asked perceptively.

As the Crowman answered, Sergeant Beetroot slipped into a back room and emerged pushing a vast, sixteen-wheeled trolley with a massive, towering wedding cake perched precariously on it, tier upon tier of icing and marzipan and currants rising up towards the roof. There was a gasp of admiration from the scarecrows.

'Indeed it has, Aunt Sally. At every scarecrow wedding, the wedding feast commences with the ceremony of Throwing The Wedding Cake. And this is traditionally led by the best scarecrow and the chief bridesmaid.'

Worzel Gummidge's eyes lit up. 'Throwin' the cake, your eminence?' he breathed rapturously. 'You means me an' Aunt Sally can chuck all that there cake at each other?'

'Oh, *bliss!*' squeaked Aunt Sally, clapping her hands.

'Not all of it,' the Crowman smiled, 'You must let the bride and groom have a look in!'

'I should think so!' cried Saucy Nancy.

'Bags I the marzipan!' chimed in Cousin Cobber.

Little Pickles wormed his way to the front, through the throng of scarecrow legs, and tugged at his uncle's sleeve. 'Can I throw the top tier, Uncle Worzel?' he begged.

'Throw the top tier!' Worzel cried, aghast. 'Certainly not! You ain't big enough for throwin' top tiers, so you ain't. If anyone's throwin' the top tier it's Worzel!' and he wrenched off the top tier and hurled it at Aunt Sally. 'Cop this, you bundle o' firewood!' he bellowed.

The ceremony of Throwing The Wedding Cake had begun! Aunt Sally was ecstatically happy, screaming 'And *you* cop *this*, you horse's nosebag!' as she heaved a layer back at the scarecrow.

'Let the dog see the rabbit, then,' called Cobber Gummidge, elbowing his way to the front in best Australian fashion. 'Cop *this*, you pair o' nutcrackers!'

Saucy Nancy was at his side, 'Get this in your mush,' she laughed in her mahogany voice, 'you landlubbing haystack!'

In seconds the room was afly with cake and jelly and trifle and cream as the company got into full swing.

The Crowman slipped prudently away, and John and Sue, after a quick conspiratorial glance, dived eagerly into the mêlée and began heaving and hurling with the best of them.

'This is the best wedding I've ever been to!' gasped Sue, wiping cream from her eyes.

'Me too!' agreed John from the thickest of the fray.

There was a harsh violin chord: the scarecrows froze and looked up to a gallery where the Crowman stood with his battered old fiddle. 'Friends, friends!' he called. 'Take your places for the Scarecrow Hop!'

There was a loud cheer; and the scarecrows lined up around the room, and in a moment were dancing for all they were worth, dancing as though they would dance for ever.

Heard about the Puffin Club?

... it's a way of finding out more about Puffin books and authors, of winning prizes (in competitions), sharing jokes, a secret code, and perhaps seeing your name in print! When you join you get a copy of our magazine, *Puffin Post*, sent to you four times a year, a badge and a membership book.

For details of subscription and an application form, send a stamped addressed envelope to:

The Puffin Club Dept A
Penguin Books Limited
Bath Road
Harmondsworth
Middlesex UB7 ODA

and if you live in Australia, please write to:

The Australian Puffin Club
Penguin Books Australia Limited
P.O. Box 257
Ringwood
Victoria 3134